SHROUD OF CANVAS

Rosalind, a young widow with a daughter, has married Geoffrey Lennard after a whirlwind romance. She receives a telephone call from an unknown woman—and realises that she has married a stranger. The caller is Anne Winter, once Geoffrey's fiancée. She disappeared for seventeen years—why is she back now? And why has she contacted Geoffrey instead of her own family?

Before these questions can be answered, Anne's murdered body is found hidden in Geoffrey's garden. The police investigation begins, inexorably dragging in Geoffrey. Rosalind's faith in him does not waver. Other people knew Anne Winter, and one of them wanted rid of her. But which one?

SHROUD OF CANVAS

Isobel Lambot

·BLACK·
DAGGER
·CRIME·

First published 1967
by
Robert Hale Limited
This edition 1997 by Chivers Press
published by arrangement with
the author

ISBN 0 7451 8706 4

British Library Cataloguing in Publication Data available

Printed and bound in Great Britain by
Redwood Books, Trowbridge, Wiltshire

FOREWORD

DURING THE COURSE of a long and varied writing career, Isobel Lambot has produced over twenty crime novels and political thrillers. She trained as a teacher and later, after her marriage, she travelled widely, in Third World countries as well as in Europe. The many strands of her rich and interesting life have nourished her writing and provided her with fascinating backgrounds for her books; the people she has met have enabled her to create memorable characters—notably, the flamboyant White Russian exile on whom she based her Commissaire Orloff, the series detective featuring so splendidly in her later books.

Her earlier crime novels, of which *Shroud of Canvas* is one, are characterised by a plain, straightforward style and a confident voice. This enables her, with no wasted words, to tell a clear story and keep it moving forwards at a good pace. There is faultless craftsmanship in the way the plot is handled, with surprises deftly inserted to maintain the suspense, clues for the astute reader to pick up, red herrings to baffle just when the suspect appears obvious, and a taut storyline to keep the reader guessing as to the true identity of the perpetrator until the very end.

Isobel Lambot's characters are clearly observed and revealed by skilful thumbnail sketches and many shrewd and felicitously-expressed observances. When she says, for instance: 'The tears washed streaks into the thick make-up on her face, revealing the haggard truth beneath,' we need little more to envisage the character before us. Her dialogue is easy-flowing, never tiresome, carrying the tale along in a fluid and readable way, and *Shroud of Canvas*, the story of a man inescapably caught up as a suspect in a murder, is no exception to all this.

Lennard Plastics is a small, mainly family firm, whose members are all connected either by blood, marriage or long friendship, a hitherto happy working environment now threatened with takeover and the ugly spectre of industrial espionage. The story of the murder which erupts into the middle of this is carried along against a background of office politics and power struggles, with past enmities and present jealousies revealing themselves as the murder enquiry progresses.

The chief suspect is Geoffrey Lennard, and the story is presented mainly through the eyes of his new wife, whose fragile happiness is threatened by a disturbing telephone call, hinting at secrets in her husbands past. The consequent dark hints of indiscretions are quickly followed by the discovery of the body of Geoffrey's ex-fiancée, and actions in his past life are suddenly open to question. His wife Rosalind, as well as the police, begin to see that he is not as open and honest as he seems, either in regard to his past or in his present actions. She sees the new-found stability of herself and her young daughter slipping away as the police delve deeper, and doubts of her husband's probity increase.

Enormous changes have taken place over the last three decades in the detection of crime, and the public, through the media, is very much aware of how a murder investigation is conducted, and of the teamwork involved. Thirty years ago, when the book was written, in the days when Scotland Yard was called in to solve every major crime, there was a much more leisurely approach, and much of the enjoyment of classic crime novels is centred in the traditional sergeant/senior detective partnership. Here, in *Shroud of Canvas*, we have a particularly happy combination—a sergeant who is anxious to prove his worth, but who is not simply a foil for his brilliant superior officer, and one who has, moreover, more than a passing interest in the case on which he finds himself working. Longton, the superintendent in charge of the case, is tough, shrewd and makes his mind up fairly early on who the culprit is. The author has not, however, fallen into the facile trap of making him stubborn and blinkered, although his earlier certainties may make him appear so at first. He is, in fact, open-minded and when the facts prove him wrong, is willing to admit it.

The book ends with a denouement in all the best traditions of the classic detective story, with the closed circle of suspects gathered together to hear the surprising revelation of who the real murderer is.

Shroud of Canvas is a story to appeal to all those who appreciate a well-told, readable and credible piece of crime fiction from an author who continues to give pleasure to new readers and old alike.

MARJORIE ECCLES

THE BLACK DAGGER CRIME SERIES

The Black Dagger Crime series is a result of a joint effort between Chivers Press and a sub-committee of the Crime Writers' Association, consisting of Marian Babson, Peter Chambers, Peter Lovesey and Sarah J. Mason. It is designed to select outstanding examples of every type of detective story, so that enthusiasts will have the opportunity to read once more classics that have been scarce for years, while at the same time introducing them to a new generation who have not previously had the chance to enjoy them.

SHROUD OF CANVAS

ROSALIND was alone in the house when the first call came. She was standing at the window of her bedroom, watching the sturdy figure of Mrs Purvis receding down the lane. Below her was the garden—or rather, what would be the garden, in time—and the new white fence which separated it from the narrow country road. Near the gate was a heap, covered by a tarpaulin. The builders' stuff, waiting for collection, now that the job of converting the old barn into a comfortable house was done.

Mrs Purvis had reached the bend now, and would be out of sight in a moment. She was a grand worker, that woman. A treasure. They had been lucky to find her. But Rosalind was glad to see her go. She loved to have the house to herself.

The house. . . . Oh, it was so much more than just a house. It was the Promised Land, the haven after the storm, the unexpected refuge where she and Sally had found shelter.

The telephone broke into her thoughts.

Rosalind ran downstairs, wondering who could be calling them. There was still a thrill for her, each time she heard the brisk ringing of the phone, or the doorbell. She was *someone* now, a woman with a place in society, not a nameless waif in the vast uncomprehending city.

It might be one of her in-laws, Geoffrey's mother, or Glenda. Or maybe, Mrs Winter : she had left a coffee invitation dangling the last time they met in the village. Or perhaps Geoffrey had forgotten something. Or he might be ringing just for the pleasure of hearing her voice. . . .

"Parrington 246."

For a moment no one answered, and Rosalind had time to wonder if it was a wrong number.

"Parrington 246," she repeated.

"Who is speaking, please?"

The voice was soft, unknown. A woman. And uncertain, as though the caller was disconcerted to be answered by another woman.

"This is Rosalind Lennard. Who is calling?"

There was another hesitation.

"I wanted to speak to Mr Geoffrey Lennard. Is he there?"

"I'm afraid not. I'm Mrs Lennard. Can I take a message?"

This time there was a long silence. Rosalind wondered if the caller had hung up.

"Are you there?"

"Yes, I'm here. Did you say you were Mrs Lennard? Geoffrey's wife?"

"Yes, that's right. What do you want?"

But there was no reply. Only a sharp click as the caller put down her receiver.

Rosalind stood there, stupidly, holding the telephone to her ear, but the uncompromising *brrr* told her that she was wasting her time.

It was an odd sensation, like stepping off an edge. One moment, the foot was on firm ground, the next finding only empty air and a sickening lurch.

She had no time to explore her reactions. There was the sound of a car turning into the gate and bumping over the rough drive. Rosalind replaced the receiver, and went to the front door.

The car was a smart white Triumph, and out of it there emerged a slender figure, clad in a white dress.

White suits a blonde.

And it did, thought Rosalind, almost grudgingly, as her eyes took in that shining head.

The whole turn-out was immaculate.

"Hallo, Glenda," she called.

Glenda Hardwick, Geoffrey's half-sister, picked her way between little pools of water to the porch.

"When's the drive being done?" she complained, "it's absolutely foul."

"It rained a bit this morning," Rosalind reminded her, "you should see it when there's a downpour."

"Thanks," said Glenda with a shudder, "I don't want to. Have the builders finished?"

"Yes, thank heavens. But they've left no end of stuff here. The contractor can't start on the drive until they have moved it. But their lorry's in dock, or something, so it will have to wait till next week."

"Sickening," murmured Glenda, stepping back carefully to glance along the front of the building.

"They've made rather a good job of it," said Rosalind, with shy pride.

"Not bad, as these things go, but it wouldn't suit me," replied Glenda frankly, "I can't bear old houses."

Rosalind had to remind herself quite sharply that she would *not* be upset by anything Glenda said. She and Geoffrey loved the place, and, after all, they had to live in it, not Glenda. And it would be useless to retort that they wouldn't live in Glenda's modern monstrosity if they were paid to do it.

She forced a laugh.

"Aren't you coming in?"

Glenda stepped delicately into the hall, and followed Rosalind into the drawing room. It was a big airy room, taking up half the floor of the original barn, and looking out over the vast sweep of the flat Thanet countryside.

"I hope they won't decide to build at the bottom of your garden," Glenda said sharply.

"They won't," replied Rosalind placidly, "Geoffrey has bought the farm, too." She was rewarded by the look of baffled spite on her sister-in-law's face.

"Let's have some tea," she suggested, and led her guest back through the hall, into the bright modern kitchen. Glenda followed her, taking everything in, but, by now, saying nothing.

"I thought I would have the little room at the end of the hall for a sewing room," Rosalind chattered on, "but Geoffrey has collared it, for his study. He often brings work home, you know."

"So does Edward," snapped Glenda, "I can't see why he should have to. I should have thought the company could have afforded to pay for a decent assistant for him."

This might be it, thought Rosalind warily. The reason for Glenda's visit. She never came here just to look at the house. She wants me to speak to Geoffrey for Edward. Well, she's out of luck. Edward Hardwick can fight his own battles.

"There's bound to be a lot of work at the moment," she pointed out, "with the board meeting the day after tomorrow."

"Oh, that," said Glenda, and dismissed it.

It would have been a relief, Rosalind was thinking, if she could have discussed it with Glenda. After all, she was Geoffrey's own flesh and blood, and they were all in it together. If the company went broke, they were all on the bread line. But it wasn't possible. She just didn't trust Glenda.

The kettle boiled and she made the tea.

"Sally will be home from school, soon," she said, to make conversation.

"She and Geoffrey getting on all right?" asked Glenda.

"Oh, yes. She took to him, from the first, you know."

Rosalind was glad that she had to busy herself with the tray. It wasn't an outright lie. Sally did hit it off with her step-father. But there was a problem there, all the same.

"I never thought Geoffrey would marry," Glenda was saying.

Rosalind knew that she was telling the absolute truth. She wondered if Glenda would also admit that she had counted on Geoffrey's money being hers in due time. Her sister-in-law, with her sometimes paralysing tactlessness, was quite capable of it.

"Because of Anne," Glenda added.

Rosalind's heart missed a beat.

"Anne?"

"Oh, Geoffrey hasn't told you about her? No, I don't suppose he would. He took it very badly."

"I didn't imagine for a moment that I was Geoffrey's first love," said Rosalind steadily. "He's thirty-nine and, until six months ago, he didn't know I existed. It would be very odd indeed if he had never had a girl friend. I have never asked him. It is nothing to do with me. And the same thing applies in my case. He knows that I have been married before, but he doesn't ask me questions about poor Dick."

"Anne didn't *die*," replied Glenda. "They were engaged, but she broke it off. Of course, it is a long time ago now. Sixteen or seventeen years, I should think. I don't remember much of Anne. I can't have been more than eight or nine at the time. Geoffrey used to have a photograph of her in his bedroom. It was there for years. She was Anne Winter, you know. Colonel Winter's daughter."

"I didn't know they had a daughter. I thought Giles was their only child."

"Oh, no, but no one mentions Anne."

"Why ever not?"

Glenda shrugged.

"I don't know. Anyway, that's all ancient history. He's married you, and he couldn't have picked anyone less like Anne. She was one of those little fair people, with great brown eyes."

While I am a big, strapping black-headed wench, thought Rosalind, a shade grimly. Like many tall women, she had a secret envy of small ones, and tended to discount her splendid figure and the striking contrast of her hair and green eyes.

"Don't let's talk about her," Glenda went on, "I was wondering if you and Geoffrey would come over to dinner one day next week. If he can spare the time."

"Thank you. If Edward isn't too busy," replied Rosalind politely.

The shaft mis-fired.

"He does need that assistant," said Glenda sweetly, "we shall have to talk to Geoffrey, you and I."

Rosalind was left with the impression that she had played neatly into Glenda's hands, as she was meant to do. She was so annoyed that she forgot all about the phone call.

CHAPTER 2

GEOFFREY LENNARD was standing at the window of his office, staring out and seeing nothing. He was a large man, with dark hair unstreaked by the years, and cool grey eyes set in a determined face. He was formidable— until he smiled. He would have been surprised to know how many hearts had fluttered at that smile.

The sprawl of buildings which housed Lennard Plastics lay before him, one-storey sheds in neat rows to the wire mesh of the perimeter. A couple of vans were turning out past the watchman's office and through the gate, the name of the firm painted boldly in black on their red sides. A heavily laden lorry was waiting in the road for them to clear the gateway before it drove in. A fork-lift truck buzzed briskly between a couple of buildings directly below his window. In front of the administration block, a new building in itself, where his office and the board room occupied the best part of the first floor, stood a line of cars, his own Bentley among them.

It was a long way from the Nissen hut where he and David Kindersley had started it all, here on this spot, fifteen years ago. Then the place had been a stretch of waste land, useless for farming, too far from the sea for a holiday camp or park for the summer visitors, an area which the council of the seaside town of Broadgate had marked down hopefully as a site for industrial development.

Geoffrey was thinking that he was in danger of losing it all.

He pulled himself out of his torpor and went back to his desk. He rang for his secretary.

She came in, a middle-aged woman, who had been the first clerical staff he had hired. Then it had been part-time, to do a bit of typing and bookkeeping in the garden shed which had served as an office. Then she had been a little slip of a thing with bright red hair. Now it was grey and her waist had thickened, but the warmth of her smile was undiminished.

Geoffrey started to give her a list of things he wanted doing, then changed his mind.

"Sit down, Elsie," he said.

Elsie Summers sat. She knew him too well to offer any comment.

"What are we going to do about it?" he asked, after a moment.

"There's not much we can do, before the board meeting," she replied directly.

"No," agreed Geoffrey glumly, then burst out: "If only we knew who was responsible!"

Miss Summers shrugged. Lennard Plastics was as much her life as it was Geoffrey's. If he was pushed out, she wouldn't stay either. Stanley Threadwell or whatever stooge he put in charge could find another confidential secretary.

"We may never find out. We must just be more careful in the future. We have been lucky that it has never happened before."

"I don't like to think that one of our people is a traitor," he replied.

"We're not the first firm to have a secret pinched, and

I don't suppose we shall be the last. And we don't know how they got hold of it."

Geoffrey's mouth tightened.

"One of us told them. Took them the drawings for them to copy."

Miss Summers shook her head.

"Not necessarily. You hear all sorts of funny things nowadays, about industrial spying. Microfilms and what-not. They employ professionals."

Geoffrey refused to be comforted.

"The fact remains, Elsie, that our keenest rival got hold of the design of our new food storage containers, before we even applied for the patent. And they've got them out on the market before us. So *ours* are going to look like the copy. And worse, *they've* patented the thing. They'll make a killing before we've even started. I can't blame Threadwell for being enraged."

Miss Summers sniffed.

"Him? It's a great pity we had to let him on to the board."

"We couldn't keep him out," Geoffrey reminded her, "he controls a devil of a lot of shares. Our mistake was to turn ourselves into a public company. We should have stayed as we were. We might not have made so much money but at least we should have kept the business in our own hands. Oh, well, it's too late now for that. We had better get some work done."

Miss Summers consulted her notebook.

"The Colonel wanted to have a word with you, but he says it isn't important. There's an argument going on between the mechanics and the van drivers, but he thinks he can sort it out. I gather that Tom Yates isn't being very co-operative."

"He wouldn't be!" muttered Geoffrey, thinking momentary evil of the garage foreman. "Anything else?"

"No. But you haven't forgotten that Mr Threadwell is coming in at four?" she added diffidently.

Geoffrey snorted.

"I have not. I'll have to cool my head before I can face that sanctimonious old devil. Hold the fort, Elsie. I'm going for a stroll round."

Outside, the corridor was deserted. The shining floor was bare, the neatly-labelled doors shut. Behind each one people were working. Geoffrey wondered who were friends and who foes. It was not a pleasant thought in a factory which he had created out of his own hard work.

He stepped forward, trying to shake himself out of the mood. Further down the corridor, a door opened and a slim, youthful figure appeared. The young man glanced casually about him, stopping abruptly when he saw Geoffrey.

"You going out, sir?"

"Only into the works for a while, Giles."

"Mr Threadwell is coming," Giles Winter added, a shade nervously. There was a quality about Geoffrey Lennard which disturbed him. He could not define it. Geoffrey was a commanding figure, but so was Giles's own father. Colonel Winter had been a good and efficient soldier, but he lacked the unnerving sense of power which Giles found in Geoffrey. Even a couple of years as Geoffrey's personal assistant had not accustomed Giles to it. It was one of the things which made Giles hate the very name of the factory.

"No, I haven't forgotten," Geoffrey assured him, and went on down the corridor. Then Giles heard his feet hurrying down the stairs.

Giles Winter looked after him for a moment, before stepping across to the door in front of him. He knocked. A voice called to him to come in.

"You free for a moment, Edward?"

Behind his desk, Edward Hardwick, the company secretary, shuffled with his papers.

"I'm busy, Giles," he complained.

He was a thin man, in his thirties, with a perpetual

air of worry hanging over him. He was the very embodiment of a conscientious hard-working accountant. He wore thick, pebble-lensed glasses. From behind these, his eyes looked shrewdly at Giles.

"What do you want now?"

"Nothing much," said Giles, "just some notes his lordship has made out for you for the board meeting."

"You're not very respectful."

Giles laughed.

"I wouldn't call him that to *anyone*, Edward. Only to those I trust. You wouldn't split on me, would you, Edward?"

"I'm glad you trust me," replied Edward seriously, "but you should be more careful. Everyone isn't to be trusted, you know. And Geoffrey could make it hot for you."

"I'm sick of being grateful to Geoffrey," muttered Giles, "anyone would think employing me was a charity."

"Geoffrey is a very generous man," said Edward, "but if you cross him, you'll find that he will be quite ruthless. And the families being old friends won't do any good either. One thing you can be thankful for: he won't believe ill of anyone until the truth is pushed in front of his nose."

"Meaning what?"

But Edward shook his head.

"I shouldn't have said that. But it makes me mad to see a fine man like Geoffrey being deceived."

"Come on," Giles coaxed him, "you can tell me. You know I won't blab. And I am Geoffrey's P.A. I ought to know what is going on."

Edward hesitated.

"It's not about the business," he said reluctantly.

Giles stared.

"But there's nothing—oh, you can't mean— *Rosalind*?"

Edward nodded unhappily.

"I never thought he would lose his head over a woman," he confessed. "I don't mean that he should not have married. I have thought for a long time that he needed a wife. But to marry a girl that no one knows anything about—after knowing her only a month or two !"

Giles shrugged.

"Rosalind's all right."

Edward pursed his lips.

"She may be. But there's that child. And we've only her word for it that she was *married*."

Geoffrey returned to his office in a worse temper than when he left it. He had looked in at the garage, and heard Tom Yates' side of the difference of opinion with Colonel Winter. It had the makings of a first-class row, if mis-handled. He made a mental note to have a word with George Winter. He was a grand old boy and he ran the personnel office like clockwork, but a man like Tom Yates was bound to raise all the old soldier in him.

Geoffrey put his head into Miss Summers' office. He wasn't pleased to see Peter Maynard lounging on a corner of her desk. Peter, Geoffrey's junior by five years, was an outdoor type, bronzed and fit, but today, his usually springy brown hair looked limp, his blue eyes watery.

"Waiting for me, Peter?"

Peter nodded.

"I'm busy," said Geoffrey shortly. Peter was an astonishingly good salesman, and he owed his position as sales director to that, rather than to the fact that he was Geoffrey's cousin. But this afternoon, he was the last person Geoffrey wanted to see. In two days' time, Peter might find himself facing a difficult choice. If there was an open rift between Geoffrey and Stanley Threadwell, Peter, like the other directors, would have to decide whom to support. And Peter was engaged to Threadwell's daughter. . . .

Geoffrey wanted to postpone the moment when Peter would tell him of his decision. Left alone with him now, he might even be daft enough to ask him. . . .

"Take yourself away from here," Geoffrey advised him. "Threadwell's due in a few minutes. He'll throw a fit if he finds you interrupting. You know what he is like."

Peter raised a hand in salute and went.

"He's in a difficult position," Miss Summers offered, gently. "He'll hate having to side against you, but if he doesn't support that man, he'll lose Lucille. Mr Thread-well is quite capable of forbidding the marriage."

"Not to mention cutting Lucille off without a penny," added Geoffrey.

"You can't blame Peter for not wanting to lose all that money. He's not marrying Lucille *for* it, but it would be most unfair if she didn't inherit from her father. I never have believed that people genuinely preferred love in a garret."

Geoffrey was forced to laugh.

"You're right, of course. Get David for me, will you?"

He went through into his own room to wait.

David Kindersley followed hard on his heels. He was a sturdy figure, with rumpled fair hair and direct blue eyes. His face was flushed with temper.

Geoffrey raised his brows.

"You were quick."

"I was on my way to see you. Geoffrey, Seldon's driving me crazy."

"What's he doing now?"

David caught the weary note in his old friend's voice.

"Forget it!" he said tersely, "it's a chronic condition, anyway. I'll go and let off steam elsewhere. What can I do for you?"

Geoffrey slumped in his chair. In front of David, he could relax.

"What will you do if Threadwell forces the issue?"

David laughed.

"Just let him try it. We're all behind you, Geoffrey."

"I wish I could believe that."

"You still haven't a clue who did it?"

Geoffrey shook his head.

"No. And I don't suppose we shall find out now. It happened months ago. And how many people knew about those drawings? Only the board, and a few of the staff. All people I'd trust with my life."

"Perhaps it was Threadwell himself, to create trouble."

Geoffrey looked up swiftly.

"I'd be glad to believe that, David, but can you honestly see him doing himself out of a substantial profit?"

"Not unless he has shares in the other firm," retorted David. "I think I'll look into that. It might give me a bit of mud to sling myself at the board meeting. Thanks very much. It will take my mind off Seldon and his antics."

It was illogical to feel so much cheered. Much as he disliked the man, Geoffrey knew that Threadwell would never involve himself so blatantly.

But David had put new heart into him. David, the old ally, who could be relied on in any moment of need. David, who had come to him for relief from the difficulties of working with Richard Seldon, whose inclusion in the company was Geoffrey's work.

He couldn't imagine what it would be like to be without David.

A moment later, Miss Summers ushered in his expected and unwelcome visitor.

Stanley Threadwell was an imposing man, running to fat now, with sharp eyes peering out of the folds of flesh of his face. He extended a well-manicured hand.

"Well, Lennard," he said, "who did it? Or was it yourself?"

CHAPTER 3

GLENDA HARDWICK's car had scarcely turned out of the unmade drive before Sally came hopping up it, following a devious route so that not one of the muddy patches was missed out. From the front door, Rosalind, as yet unnoticed, watched her progress, the young, intent face concentrating on each calculated hop to leap the morass and land safely on the other side. The rich brown pony-tail bobbed about the neat little head with each jump.

At nine years old, Sally bore a marked resemblance to her father. Facially—but not in character, thought Rosalind grimly, not if I can help it. Dick Johnson had had charm, all right, but little else to commend him.

Sally looked up.

"Hallo, Mummy!"

The rest of the way was taken at a run.

"Sorry I'm late but Diane's mummy wanted to call at the post office, and she met someone, and they talked for *hours*." She ran into the hall, pulling off her coat as she went. "Your turn to take us tomorrow, Mummy."

Rosalind felt a catch in her throat and wondered if she would ever get used to the wonderful ordinariness of things here at Parrington. Taking her turn with two other mothers who lived locally to run their daughters to school in Broadgate. Shopping in the village and gossiping in the post office. Just being here and knowing that Geoffrey would soon be home from the factory.

No more fighting. No more wondering how Sally would manage if anything happened to her. No more regretting the wasted years.

Sally followed her into the kitchen.

"I'm starving, Mummy. We had prunes for pudding today. Absolutely foul. I didn't want to eat mine but

Miss West made me. What time will *he* be home?"

Rosalind, busy cutting bread and butter, cast her daughter a look of exasperation. She put down the knife.

"You'll have to decide what you are going to call him, Sally. We can't go on like this."

"It's a bit awkward," said Sally defensively.

"You like him, don't you?"

"Oh, yes, you know I do. He's fun."

Rosalind took up the knife again and bent to her task.

"Well, then. Couldn't you manage 'Daddy'?"

Sally shook her head vigorously.

"Oh, no, Mummy, not that."

Rosalind reflected that she had only herself to thank for it. Over the years, to bolster Sally's courage and her own, she had built up a totally fictitious picture of Dick.

"Uncle Geoffrey, then?" she suggested.

But Sally wouldn't commit herself.

"I'll think about it," she said.

They were interrupted by a short blast on a car horn. Sally ran to the window.

"It's him!" she cried and ran out to meet Geoffrey.

He's early, thought Rosalind, with a sudden twinge of fear. What would bring him home so early when he is snowed under with work for the board meeting?

Outside, Geoffrey was driving solemnly round to the garage, Sally in the passenger seat. It had become a habit—almost a ritual with them—they did it daily. Geoffrey would sound his horn as he turned in at the gate, then wait for Sally to join him for the trip to the garage. And on the way from the garage to the house, they would pause to look at the rabbit which Geoffrey had given to the child the day they moved into the house.

Geoffrey appeared at the kitchen door alone. One glimpse of his face confirmed Rosalind's fears. She went into his arms, crying, "Darling, what's wrong?"

He held her for a moment, then sighed and let her go.

"Sally's feeding the rabbit," he said.

But Rosalind would not be put off.

"Geoffrey, what is it? What has happened?"

"I've made a fool of myself, Roz. Threadwell put my back up and I let him have it. It was all I could do not to knock his teeth down his throat. I lost my temper with him and told him a few home truths."

Rosalind's face cleared.

"Is that all? I should think it would do him the world of good. Someone should have done it years ago."

Geoffrey shook his head.

"Men like Threadwell can't take it. He'll never forgive it or forget it. He's out for control of the company. This is just one more nail in my coffin."

"But he can't push you out. You built it up. You and David."

"The trouble is, he can. We laid ourselves open to this when we became a public company. The shareholders have the last word. If they aren't satisfied with the board of directors, they can throw us out."

"But I thought you had guarded against that. Haven't you control of the majority of the shares?"

Geoffrey sighed.

"On paper, yes. But only if we all stick together."

Rosalind stared at him.

"You mean, some of the others mightn't support you? I can't believe that, Geoffrey. Threadwell is the only stranger on the board. The others were directors when it was still a private company. They wouldn't let Threadwell push you out."

"I wish I could believe that. It's my own fault. I should have seen the writing on the wall when Threadwell started buying all the available shares. Now he has a twenty per cent holding in his own name, which is as much as I have and more than any other director. There's fifteen per cent of the shares in other hands, and heaven knows how many of those votes Threadwell controls."

"But at the worst that's only thirty-five per cent."

"Plus Peter's five per cent."

"Peter!" Rosalind exclaimed. "He's your cousin; he's been with the firm for years. He'd never let you down."

"Lucille," Geoffrey reminded her, briefly.

"Oh, yes, of course. But even so!"

"Peter will have to keep in with Threadwell. It's no good blinking at the fact, Roz."

"All right, then. That's forty per cent. It still doesn't give him enough votes in a shareholders' meeting to oust you."

Geoffrey did not reply for a moment.

Then: "As long as the others all support me," he said heavily.

"Of course they will."

"There's no 'of course' about it, Roz. Threadwell knows what he is doing. He's going to play this business of the information leak for all he is worth. He can't fail. The shareholders have a right to be angry about it. We've spent a huge sum on machines and retooling for this new line, only to be pipped at the post by our closest rival."

"It couldn't just be a coincidence, could it? People do sometimes have the same ideas at the same time."

Geoffrey shook his head.

"Not a hope. They got hold of a copy of our drawings, all right. I've been making a few inquiries of my own."

"But it's stealing," Rosalind protested. "Can't you take them to court?"

"We can't prove a thing. And they beat us to it at the patents office. We would be flogging a dead horse."

"So what will happen?"

"We shall soon find out," said Geoffrey bitterly, "at the board meeting. My guess is that Threadwell will call for a general meeting of shareholders. To discuss the present management's responsibility for the situation. If he can get that motion passed by the board, we can be certain that he will persuade the shareholders to vote in a new lot of directors."

"But how could he get it passed by the board? Even with Peter, that's only two votes and there are seven of you."

"He's glib. And the only ones I can be sure of are David and Edward."

"But Colonel Winter," said Rosalind, appalled, "he wouldn't—"

"I can't be sure," Geoffrey cut in, "and he has that ninny Giles to look for. Threadwell might offer him some bait. That gives him a possible three votes. Which leaves Richard Seldon in the position of casting vote."

"But he's your godfather."

"He's also nursing a grievance. He's never forgiven me for buying up his rotten little business, nor for giving him a job in the firm, which he can't hold down, and a seat on the board which makes him a menace at every meeting. I don't imagine Threadwell will have much trouble with him."

"But, Geoffrey," cried Rosalind, "it's unbelievable. I won't believe it."

"You may have to—after Thursday," he said dryly.

The ringing of the phone broke the tension between them. Geoffrey went to answer it. Rosalind, her mind full of fears for Geoffrey and the business, hovered in the kitchen doorway.

It was bad news. She knew it was bad news.

Geoffrey was taking the call on the extension in the study. She could hear nothing from where she stood, only the occasional word from him. At last she could bear it no longer. She tiptoed across the hall to the other instrument.

She had never listened in on a conversation before. She was ashamed of herself, but she just had to know— this minute.

It was a shock to recognise the quiet voice of the caller of earlier in the afternoon.

The woman was saying, "It's very good of you, Geoffrey."

And Geoffrey replied, "Think nothing of it, Anne. It's the least I can do."

Anne!

Rosalind replaced the receiver quietly. She stole back to the kitchen. From the study, she heard Geoffrey hang up. In a moment, he would come to her and tell her that he had just had such a surprise. An old friend had rung up and. . . .

And what?

She didn't know.

Geoffrey put his head round the kitchen door.

"That was David, Roz. He needs me at the works. I shan't be any longer than I can help."

*　　*　　*

David Kindersley's office was labelled "Technical Director" and occupied one end of a production shed, handy for the machines and for the laboratory. Nothing could tempt David into the smart room in the new office block, which he had been allotted. He wanted to keep his hand firmly on the production lines, all the more because he had Richard Seldon as his production manager. Seldon's office lay next to his. Now it was another source of friction between the two men, for Seldon wanted to move into the new block.

They were arguing the point, for the dozenth time that week. Seldon was in his sixties, a grey man with unkempt hair and untidy clothes. A battered pipe was wedged habitually in one corner of his mouth, but it was usually unlit.

"It's all of a piece," Seldon was grumbling, "with the way I'm treated round here. Anyone would think I was the office boy instead one of the directors. I was running a factory before you were born."

"If it means that much to you," returned David shortly, "take yourself off into the new block. But don't waste any more of my time. I don't care what you do."

"You know quite well I can't do that, not if you're still staying here. It would look funny."

"No more funny than the spectacle of a production manager who sticks in his office all day and never sets foot on the factory floor," snapped David, his temper getting the better of him.

"I might know you would descend to insults when you can't hold your own in an argument," said Seldon huffily, and went out, banging the door behind him.

David ground his teeth. He was furious that he had let himself be provoked. Now he supposed he would have to apologise to the old basket.

There was a knock on the door.

Perhaps it was Richard Seldon back again.

"Come in. Oh, it's you, Geoffrey."

Geoffrey shut the door behind him.

"What have you been doing to Richard? He's wearing his noble, martyred look."

David grinned suddenly.

"He's got me just where he wants me. He gets me to lose my temper then goes around like that until I've apologised. I can't handle him, Geoffrey."

Geoffrey did not smile at it.

"It's my fault, David. I was the one who thought he could do a useful job in the factory. When we bought him out we should have given him his seat on the board and nothing else. I should have known he would be a pain in the neck. He's so damned incompetent it's a wonder he hung on as long as he did, on his own."

"He's not so bad as all that," David said fairly. "He'd be all right if he hadn't such an inflated idea of his own importance. The men like him, too—on the few occasions when he shows his face. Ah, let's forget him. These things are sent to try us—and they do! How's it going, Geoffrey?"

"What?"

"The doings for the meeting, of course."

"Oh, that. I wasn't thinking of that. Something very odd has happened, David."

They were interrupted. It was Peter Maynard.

"There you are, Geoffrey," he began, and then pulled out his handkerchief to sneeze into it.

"Good heavens, Peter," said David, "where did you pick up that cold?"

Peter looked up.

"I was out in the boat the other day and got a ducking. Didn't think a thing about it. Now this."

"And didn't bother about sitting around in wet clothes, either," commented David. "Young idiot."

"Did you want me, Peter?" asked Geoffrey.

"I've been looking for you all over the place," Peter admitted. "To be honest, I thought I ought to go home and nurse this cold."

Geoffrey looked at him speculatively.

"Yes, Peter," he said quietly, "do that. And don't come in again until you're feeling better."

There was a tone in his voice which made David glance at him sharply.

Peter gave his cousin a wavering smile.

"Thanks, Geoffrey."

He turned towards the door.

"Wait a minute," said Geoffrey. "Now you are here, Peter, you might as well hear what I was going to tell David. I might need help from both of you. Anne Winter is here."

"Anne?" cried Peter.

"Anne?" echoed David. "Are you sure?"

Geoffrey nodded.

"She phoned me last night. I went over to meet her for a while. She's staying at the 'Old Ship', here, in Broadgate."

"What does she want?" demanded Peter.

"She wants to make it up with her family. She has asked me to help. I've promised I'll approach her father."

"Anne," murmured David, "what's she like, now?"

"Older, of course. She must be thirty-five now. And thinner. Too thin. She doesn't look very well. I understand she has been ill."

"What are you going to do?" asked Peter.

"Speak to the Colonel, of course," Geoffrey replied. "She should never have stayed away so long. Or gone in the first place for that matter. If he won't listen to me, you two will have to have a go at him. I'm sure Mrs Winter would be glad to have her daughter back. I'll see if I can catch him, now."

He went out quickly.

Peter said, "Do you think he will?"

"Who? The Colonel?"

"Yes. Have her back."

David frowned.

"If she had been my daughter I would never have let her go away. Of if she had, I'd have torn England to pieces but what I'd have found her."

Peter glanced at him shrewdly.

"You were in love with her, too, weren't you, David? Oh, I know I was only seventeen and supposed to be the young cousin who knew nothing about what was going on, but none of you fooled me. Her mother had pushed her into that engagement with Geoffrey."

"He was in love with her," said David repressively. "Look how he has never bothered with another woman until Rosalind appeared."

"He snapped her up quickly enough," said Peter, unabashed. "I say, you don't think Anne reappearing will mess things up for him, do you?"

"Why should it? Anne couldn't have made it clearer that she didn't love him, at the time."

"I thought he looked pretty upset."

Geoffrey found the Colonel in the personnel office. The place was meticulously tidy, the desks swept clean of unwanted papers, the staff industriously engaged about their business. Geoffrey passed through it, and encountered the Colonel's secretary in the doorway of his private office. She dodged hastily out of the way.

George Winter was bent over a pile of papers on his desk, but he pushed them to one side as Geoffrey came in. He was a tall, well-built man, and in his Army days had looked handsome in his uniform. Now, his sparse fair hair was spread out carefully to cover the bald patch on the top of his head, and he had to use glasses, but his eyes were still keen and shrewd.

"Ah, Geoffrey," he said.

Geoffrey hesitated.

"I wanted to have a word with you, Colonel," he began.

"About this garage thing, I suppose. Yates is being a stiff-necked fool."

"No. It wasn't that. It's something—personal."

Colonel Winter's eyebrows rose.

"Personal?"

Geoffrey looked away.

"It's about Anne. She—"

"Anne?" the Colonel broke in, "what Anne?"

Geoffrey darted a swift look at him and was not comforted to see the bleak stare of the brown eyes, which were so like Anne's.

"Anne. Your daughter."

The Colonel's hand gripped the edge of the desk. The bones of the knuckles showed white under the skin.

"My daughter?" he repeated, in icy tones. "You're mistaken, Geoffrey. I have no daughter."

CHAPTER 4

No MATTER what Rosalind did, the uncertainty enveloped her in a black cloud.

Uncertainty?

It was nothing of the sort. The fact was, Geoffrey had lied to her. He had received a telephone call which took him out of the house. He said that it was David, asking him to go back to the factory. Only, she had listened in on the conversation.

She did not know whether to be glad or sorry that she had.

She would never have questioned his word. With the present crisis at the works, she would not have wondered what was keeping him when he did not return until so late that night.

But the caller had been a woman named Anne, and it was impossible to escape the conclusion that Geoffrey had gone to meet her and had spent the evening in her company.

Perhaps it was better to know these things. . . .

Mrs Purvis called from the kitchen, "I've made a cup of tea, Mrs Lennard. It'll buck you up a bit."

Rosalind dragged herself into the kitchen. Mrs Purvis, her sturdy body clad in a flowered overall, was laying out cups on the table.

"Still got your headache?" she inquired sympathetically.

Rosalind summoned up a smile.

"I'm much better now, thank you."

But it wasn't a real headache. It was the long hours lying awake, listening to Geoffrey's steady breathing. Nothing upset his sleep, neither worries at work, nor. . . . Nor what? Guilty conscience? If only he had offered some word of explanation. . . .

She couldn't go on like this. Something had to be done.

"Mrs Purvis," she said abruptly, "you've lived here a long time, haven't you?"

The cleaning woman showed no surprise. Mrs Lennard wasn't herself this morning. Why, she hadn't even heard when she was asked if she would like some more aspirin, just now. This was no sort of reply.

"Yes," she said, "I have. It's nearly thirty years since I married Purvis and came to live here. Lived in Broadgate all my life, till then."

"Then you would have known Anne Winter?"

Rosalind was ashamed of herself. The question came out so baldly. She should, at least, have wrapped it up, worked round to it tactfully.

"Anne Winter?" echoed Mrs Purvis, astonished.

"Yes." Rosalind made an effort to pull herself together. "I never knew the Winters had a daughter. Someone told me, the other day. I wondered. I thought you might remember her."

Mrs Purvis glanced shrewdly at her employer. Village gossip had raked up the old story three months back when it became known that Geoffrey Lennard had married and was bringing his bride to live in Parrington. It looked as though some echo of it had reached Mrs Lennard herself.

"I remember her," she said steadily, "nice girl, she was. The Colonel thought the world of her."

"Does she ever visit?"

"No. She's never been back. Poor thing."

Rosalind fiddled with her tea-cup.

"What happened to her?" she asked, trying to keep her voice casual.

Mrs Purvis was not deceived. The bride had heard something. And it would be a garbled version, for no one knew the whole truth, not even Edna Purvis, for all that she was working at the 'Hall' at the time, and Miss Anne had looked on her as a friend. She would have to tell her. Miss Anne would have wanted her to. She had a sudden recollection of the pain in Anne Winter's voice the last time that she had spoken to Geoffrey Lennard.

"I should never have let the engagement be announced, Edna. I should never have let him think. . . . Oh, how can I ever undo the harm I have done?"

This was a chance. Edna Purvis could do it for her. At least, set at rest the mind of Geoffrey's wife.

But still she hesitated. The problem was how much to tell. She had kept her own counsel for so many years.

The hesitation cost her the chance.

Rosalind, waiting anxiously for Mrs Purvis to reply, heard the sound of a car outside. With a small sigh, she turned to look out of the window.

Her mother-in-law's Mini was turning into the drive.

Of all the moments for Mrs Wareham to arrive!

She went slowly to the front door.

In her youth Margaret Wareham had been a beauty, and even now, turned sixty, her figure could have been the envy of many a girl. But she made no pretence of her age. Her once-fair hair was honestly grey. She wore only the most subdued make-up.

Rosalind, watching her step gracefully out of the small car, reflected that Glenda, for all her present glamour, would be lucky if she was as attractive as her mother when she reached the same age.

But it was always difficult to believe that Mrs Wareham was Geoffrey's mother, too. They were so unlike, in every way; physically; mentally. There was a certain coldness between mother and son. "Geoffrey takes after his father" was all Mrs Wareham would say on the subject. Rosalind wondered how happy she had been with her first husband. Or with her second one, for that matter. Glenda's father had been dead for over ten years, she knew, and Mrs Wareham never spoke of him.

To Rosalind, she had been kindness itself, from the start. She had greeted her almost with relief, as if getting Geoffrey married off was her sole ambition.

"Rosalind, my dear," she cried, "you look washed out. Are you all right? You are doing too much, getting the house straight. Come home with me for the day."

Rosalind declined with a laugh. But it was kind, and it warmed her chilled soul.

"I just ran in for Sally's suitcase," Mrs Wareham was saying. "I thought it would save time tonight. You haven't forgotten she's staying with me, have you?"

Rosalind shook her head.

"I wouldn't have had a chance. Sally has been talking about her friend's party for days. But it's very kind of you to keep her with you overnight. We could easily have fetched her."

"It will be nice for you and Geoffrey to have an evening to yourselves. Besides I am doing it entirely from selfish motives. I want to have her with me." Mrs Wareham's eyes clouded over: "She's the only grandchild I have."

And Sally was looking forward to staying with Mrs Wareham almost as much as to the party. The child could not accept Geoffrey as her father, but Mrs Wareham had become "Grandma" within a matter of weeks.

They went upstairs to pack the little suitcase.

"Sally needs a family," Mrs Wareham went on, neatly folding the precious party dress, "it was unfortunate that you and Dick were both orphans."

Rosalind was glad that she was turned away from her mother-in-law, packing Sally's night-things. She felt the colour mount in her face. She hated lying, but it had become a habit. It was true enough about Dick. He had no relations she had ever heard of. But her own family. . . . That was another matter, and she had long since passed the point of no return.

It was a subject she could not discuss with anyone. There was no future in it. What's done, is done.

Margaret Wareham drove away, but by that time, Mrs Purvis, her work finished, was on her way back to the village. Rosalind had the house to herself. For once, she was not glad of it.

At four o'clock, the telephone rang.

Geoffrey's voice said, "Look, darling, I'll be late home. I don't know what time. Don't wait dinner for me."

Rosalind choked down the words which rushed to her lips, the violent demand if he was going to Anne.

"Oh, the board meeting arrangements, I suppose?" she replied, trying to keep her voice even.

Did she imagine that he hesitated?

"Yes, Roz. Don't worry. I'll be home as early as I can, but I can't say when."

*　　*　　*

There was a nightmare sense of repetition. Was she doomed to sit at the breakfast table each morning waiting for an explanation which never came? This was the second morning, although last night she had slept, heavily, as the result of the pill she had taken.

She had wandered round the silent house all the evening, waiting for the sound of Geoffrey's car, wishing one moment that Sally was not away for the night, glad at another that she was not there to witness her mother's anxiety.

Once, in desperation, she had phoned the office but there was no reply. Not that it meant anything. Geoffrey could have told the switchboard not to leave him connected with an outside line, so that he could get on with his work in peace. But if he was working late, on the agenda for the board meeting, then David would surely be there too. It had taken her half an hour to bring herself to call David's flat. There was no reply from there either, and for a while she could persuade herself that Geoffrey had told her the truth.

But the previous evening he had gone to meet Anne. . . .

At last, she had taken her pill and sunk into a deep drugged sleep, so that she had no idea when he had come home.

This morning Geoffrey looked haggard, too.

This was The Day. The board meeting was at two o'clock. . . .

They sat opposite each other, neither uttering a word. At last Geoffrey clattered his cup down on its saucer and muttered that it was time for him to go.

I'm a bad wife, thought Rosalind in sudden panic. I ought to be helping him, when he has so much worry, not sitting here wondering if he is seeing another woman. We love each other and where there is love there must be trust. He'll explain it all to me when he can, when this horrible meeting is over and done with.

She followed him out into the hall. She put her hand on his arm.

"It will be all right, Geoffrey. Don't worry. They'll support you."

He smiled briefly.

"I'm not counting on it, love."

"But they must. They *can't* let you down."

He put his arms round her.

"We'll see. There's one thing. Peter's not coming to the board meeting. He's got the 'flu. I sent him home yesterday."

"Oh, good!"

Geoffrey laughed.

"I fancy Peter is rather glad of it, too. He's in a nasty position. He doesn't want to choose between me and Threadwell. Very convenient, that cold of his. But it's genuine, all right."

"But that means that at the worst you will be three against three. You, David and Edward against Threadwell, the Colonel and Mr Seldon. And I won't believe that the Colonel will vote against you. You can't lose, Geoffrey, now."

"I can win a postponement, Roz. That's all. If Threadwell intends to force the issue with the shareholders, he will do it. If he can't get an extraordinary general meeting, he will wait till the annual one. Four months away. It's going to be a long fight."

"But you don't need to worry for today."

"No," he admitted, "not about that," he added and left her.

His parting words brought her no comfort. It all came back to—to what? To this Anne, who could make Geoffrey lie to his own wife. She must be Anne Winter. There was no one else she could be. Anne Winter, whom Geoffrey had loved so long ago.

What did she want? Why had she reappeared so suddenly?

Unless Geoffrey. . . .

Rosalind shivered. She had married a virtual stranger. Six, seven months ago, she and Sally had been living in a dingy flat in London. It was inconvenient and rather more expensive than she could afford, but it was a home. There was nowhere for Sally to play and Rosalind would not let her go in the street. Sally did not complain, but she was pale and quiet. Then suddenly, Rosalind rebelled. There was no need for her to live in London. She had no ties. Shorthand-typists were wanted everywhere.

Why, they could even live at the sea.

So she had come to Broadgate, and to Lennard Plastics.

And Geoffrey.

They had met on the stone jetty at Broadgate on a wild November day, Sally racing up and down against the wind, while she followed slowly. There wasn't another living soul in sight except the tall man leaning on the rail over the grey, rough water. A sudden squall had sent a plume of spray drenching the jetty and they had all three run for the doubtful shelter of the lighthouse. They had flattened themselves against the stone wall of the base on the leeward side, laughing.

It was natural to fall into conversation, to discover that they shared a love of wild weather and the sea. They introduced themselves by Christian names only, like children, she for fear of involvement, he, as she guessed later, for fear of his name. It was easy to slip into a habit of meeting, on the jetty or on the deserted sands, for a walk in the late afternoon, before complete darkness fell. They had fallen in love before they knew it.

Then there were the days of wonder, the days of knowing that they loved and were loved, without having so much as touched hands. They were afraid to speak of it, holding on to their dream, but knowing that it could not last, that reality would have to break in, and fearful that it would bring with it wife or husband who could not be ignored.

They had been in love two whole weeks when chance brought Rosalind from the typing pool at Lennard Plastics in response to a call from the managing director's secretary. Miss Summers set Rosalind to work at a spare desk in the corner. Ten minutes later Geoffrey walked in. . . .

In a week they were married. The succeeding months had been blissful, house-hunting, finding the barn, and converting it, getting to know each other. . . .

But there were large gaps in the knowledge. He was thirty-nine, she ten years younger. They neither wished nor were able to fill in so many years of individual experience.

There was no reason, Rosalind told herself, why Geoffrey should have told her about Anne. His past was nothing to do with her, nor was hers his affair. He had had to know about Dick, because of Sally, that was all.

But now that past was breaking in on them. Anne had come back and, whatever her purpose, she had involved Geoffrey in it. Rosalind was filled with a consuming curiosity about Anne Winter.

She looked hopefully for Mrs Purvis, but saw only a lad from the village turning in at the gate.

"Ma Purvis sent you this," he announced, when she opened the door.

A brief note informed Rosalind that Purvis's mother

had been taken ill in the night, and Mrs P. was in charge at the house for the day. She would be along in the morning if she could.

Rosalind tipped the boy, who went off whistling. He was one of the Purvis clan, and so far it meant nothing to him that his grandmother had had a stroke. But taking the note up to the "Barn" had given him an excellent excuse for being late at school.

Rosalind stifled her curiosity and set to, in the kitchen.

Later that morning, she walked the half-mile to the village. Parrington was one long street, with a couple of small side roads leading off it. The main life was on the street itself, where the shops were, and the post office, and the bus stop. At the far end, set back from the road, lay the 'Hall' where the Winters lived. Anne's old home.

Mrs Winter and Rosalind bumped into each other in the doorway of the post office. Mrs Winter was small and her hair was white, artfully tinted to suggest a platinum blonde. Her make-up was careful and too bright for a woman of her age. But, then, Daphne Winter was a woman who could not accept age, but fought it with all the means at her command. The result was disastrous.

"Rosalind, how nice to see you. Come and have coffee with me—when?—tomorrow? I must dash now. Eleven o'clock. Don't forget."

And she was gone, into her car, and away up the street. Rosalind stared after her, wondering if Anne had been to see her parents. But Mrs Winter didn't look like a woman who had recovered a long-lost daughter.

It was no good. Wherever she went, whatever she did, that morning, she could not get away from Anne.

If only she knew what Anne had looked like. If only she could visualise—

Geoffrey had had a photograph. Glenda had said that he kept it about the place for years.

It might be still around, somewhere, amongst his things. . . .

Ashamed and resolute, Rosalind went into the study, and opened Geoffrey's desk.

It was in the bottom drawer, shoved to the back, and wrapped in newspaper. It was a copy of the *Daily Post* dated the day of their first meeting on the jetty.

Rosalind was warmed by the knowledge that Geoffrey had put away his old love from the moment he met the new one. But her fingers trembled as she undid the wrappings.

She looked on the face of Anne Winter.

Outside, there was the sound of a car. Guiltily, Rosalind wrapped up the photograph and pushed it back into its hiding place. Of course, it could not be Geoffrey. It sounded more like a lorry outside, but she felt she had been caught prying.

Men were shouting to each other and the vehicle revved up. Rosalind went to the front door. The builders' lorry was backing up the unmade drive, while one of the men stood beside the dump of spare materials and directed the driver to it. Two others leapt down when it stopped and began to lift the edges of the tarpaulin covering the heap.

Rosalind went out to them.

"Morning, Missus," called the foreman, "we've got the old lorry back so we thought we'd come and move this lot for you."

Rosalind's reply was cut short by a yell from one of the men.

"Cripes!" said someone, "it's a woman."

Rosalind had time for a good look before the foreman caught her arm and pulled her back.

"Come away, Missus, you can't do her no good."

The woman was lying on the heap of planks. She was wearing a grey coat and skirt. Her eyes stared emptily at the sky.

"Reckon we'll have to ring the police," the foreman was saying. His face had gone a sickly shade, under the tan.

Rosalind nodded and stumbled towards the house. A wave of nausea swept over her and she almost fell, but she pulled herself together and went on, trying to form, in her mind, the phrases she would say to the police.

"A woman in the garden . . . dead . . . under a tarpaulin."

That would do. Better not to say that age and death could not obliterate the likeness to the photograph in the drawer in Geoffrey's desk, that it was Anne Winter.

CHAPTER 5

ELSIE SUMMERS lost her usual poise for a moment when her office door opened to admit the portly figure of Stanley Threadwell. She stared at him blankly.

"Mr Lennard in?" he inquired, but obviously only as a formality. He strode across to Geoffrey's door.

"Didn't you get my message, Mr Threadwell?" she gasped.

He turned, his hand on the door handle.

"Message?" he frowned.

"I rang round everywhere I thought you might be. They all took the message. No one knew where to find you."

He shrugged.

"I went to look over a yacht a fellow's selling at Dover. What's the message?"

"The board meeting has been postponed."

Threadwell's frown deepened.

"Postponed? Why? What's Lennard think he is playing at?"

Miss Summers tightened her lips to keep back the retort she would dearly like to have uttered.

"Mr Lennard has been called away," she said primly.

"What about?" he pressed.

Miss Summers gave up. He would have to know sooner or later. And it would be in the papers tomorrow.

"A dead body has been found in his garden."

"A dead body? What, buried?"

"No. Just lying there. The police think she was murdered."

A smile flickered over Threadwell's face but it did not reach his eyes. Miss Summers had often wondered if he ever smiled as if he really meant it. Today she was rather shocked that he should smile at all.

"So the board meeting is postponed? Not to be wondered at, in the circumstances. When's the new date?"

"Nothing has been arranged yet."

He nodded.

"Fair enough. Tell Mr Lennard not to hurry himself, Miss Summers. He is bound to have a harassing time . for the next few days. The board meeting can wait."

Miss Summers didn't like it. It didn't ring true. It wasn't in Stanley Threadwell's nature to be considerate.

"Have you any idea when Peter Maynard will be back?" he went on, and the smile was back on his face.

Miss Summers gritted her teeth. He wasn't even trying to hide the fact that it suited him to have the board meeting postponed until Peter had recovered from his cold.

"No," she said baldly.

"Lennard sent him home yesterday, didn't he?"

"Mr Maynard asked to go," she retorted, "very sensible, too. There is no point in spreading infection."

Threadwell's cold eyes glinted at her.

"Just what I always say myself, Miss Summers. But Peter should have taken to his bed days ago, when the thing came up. There was no sense in letting it develop. But for this murder, he might have missed the board meeting."

Miss Summers did not comment. It would do no good to admit that she had never seen anyone more glad to go sick than Peter Maynard.

"While I'm here, I might as well see a few people," Threadwell continued, when he saw that she was not intending to offer an opinion. "The Colonel in?"

"No, I'm afraid not."

"Don't tell me he's found a corpse in his garden too?" he asked jocularly.

Miss Summers thought it a joke in poor taste.

"There is a possibility that the poor woman is his daughter," she said repressively.

Threadwell grunted.

"Who is here, then?"

"Mr Kindersley and Mr Hardwick. Mr Seldon has gone to the hospital to see his wife. She was taken ill with appendicitis last night. As soon as he heard that the board meeting was off, he went."

"I'll have a word with Hardwick." He paused at the door. "I didn't know Colonel Winter had a daughter."

"I'm afraid I don't know anything about it," she shrugged.

Threadwell was not put out of countenance.

"It's surprising what things some of us keep hidden, isn't it, Miss Summers?" he said and went out.

Elsie Summers closed her eyes for a moment, while she fought for control. She was gripped by an unreasoning fear. He was just talking for effect, she told herself, trying to rationalise it away. He couldn't possibly *know*.

Stanley Threadwell strolled down the corridor, well pleased. Young Peter's cold had threatened to put out all his plans. Now, thanks to some unknown person who had got herself killed in Lennard's garden, things could be reorganised.

Edward Hardwick was in his office.

"You've heard?" he greeted his visitor.

Threadwell made himself comfortable in the chair in front of Hardwick's desk.

"Miss Summers has just told me. I gather the unfortunate young woman is Winter's daughter."

Edward nodded.

"So Geoffrey said, when he phoned to postpone the board meeting. He should know."

Threadwell's eyebrows rose in a question.

"He was engaged to her, years ago," Edward went on, "but it was broken off and she went away."

"And now she has turned up again in his garden, dead. Awkward for him."

Edward frowned.

"Just what are you suggesting?"

Threadwell smiled.

"Nothing. I was only thinking what the newspapers will make of it. However," he swept on before Edward could reply, "that doesn't interest me. I have no doubt that the police will find out quickly enough who is responsible. I'm more concerned with our little theft here."

"Aren't we all? It's going to mean quite a loss."

"It was a bit foolish wasn't it, ordering all the machinery before the patent had been applied for?"

Edward shook his head.

"It never occurred to us that there was any danger. Geoffrey wanted to get a head start on the thing before we publicised anything. We've worked that way for years."

"But this time the gamble didn't come off."

"No."

"Because someone in the know sold out to our biggest competitor."

Edward sighed.

"Yes," he agreed.

Threadwell's head came up sharply.

"I'm not satisfied, Hardwick. Lennard is not doing enough to find the culprit."

"He is doing everything he can. It's as much in his interest to know who it was as in anyone's," Edward said stiffly.

Threadwell leant forward.

"This is no time for blind loyalty, Hardwick. You know as well as I do that it has to be either a member of the board or one of the confidential staff. And how many does that add up to? Seven directors, and possibly their wives, and half a dozen employees. Not very much choice. There is something wrong with this company and I intend to put it right. With or without your help."

"I don't think I understand," replied Edward, in a thin voice.

But Threadwell laughed.

"Oh, yes, you do, Hardwick. And let me remind you of one thing. I'm too busy to run this place myself."

"I thought you and Seldon—" Edward began but Threadwell cut him short.

"Seldon? The man's a fool. He imagines that I shall oust Lennard and put him in command. He's in for a shock. There now, you could run to Seldon and tell him that and he might even believe you, Hardwick. And then where would I be? High and dry at the board meeting. But you won't."

Edward's eyes narrowed.

"No?"

"No," said Threadwell, "because our interests run together in this. While Geoffrey Lennard is around you will never be anything more than company secretary. And that's not enough for an ambitious man like you."

* * *

Rosalind shut the door thankfully behind the last policeman. There was still a man outside, on guard beside the dump of building materials where Anne's body had lain. But at least they were out of the house, they had asked their questions, and that was that. For the moment. She knew that they would be back soon with more questions. But she was glad of a respite, a time to collect her thoughts, a chance to talk to the others.

They were here, in the house, the people who had known Anne. Her parents, her brother, David, Peter, Mr Seldon and Geoffrey himself. They had gathered there, as the news reached them. And between them, surely they would tell her about Anne. She moved hopefully towards the drawing room door.

She walked into a dead silence. Not a silence which suddenly falls when a stranger arrives. but a well-established tense quiet. She realised that, since she had escorted the police inspector from the room, no one had spoken a word.

She looked round at them, almost as if they were strangers. Geoffrey was standing in the window, gazing out at the unfinished garden. A few yards away from him, and well separated from the others, David was on a small chair against the wall, sitting with his elbows propped on his knees, his hands together and his head down. Mrs Winter was on the settee, her son beside her. Her face was white and strained and she had been crying. Now she stared straight ahead and saw nothing. At the other end of the settee, Giles was gazing down at the folded newspaper on his knees, but he appeared to be reading the same paragraph over and over again. His father occupied an armchair beside the empty fireplace, and he too stared into space. Peter Maynard was slumped down facing him. Richard Seldon, his pipe wedged into a corner of his mouth, leant against a bookcase. He alone glanced at her as she slipped into the room.

Then Peter sneezed and the tension was broken.

"I thought you were supposed to be in bed, Peter," said Rosalind.

"I was," he replied, "but I thought I had better come, when Geoffrey phoned."

"And the best thing you can do is go back," Seldon put in.

Geoffrey turned from the window.

"There is nothing any of us can do," he said wearily.

Mrs Winter began to cry again. The tears washed fresh streaks into the thick make-up on her face, revealing the haggard truth beneath. Giles made an involuntary movement towards her, but caught himself up, glancing at his father. The Colonel gave no sign of having noticed his wife's distress.

Rosalind crossed swiftly to her side, and slipped an arm round the older woman's shoulders. Mrs Winter leant against her for a moment, while the wracking sobs diminished. Giles stood over them uncertainly. Rosalind looked up at him and read a question in his eyes.

She nodded.

"Take her home," she advised him.

Giles put out his hands and pulled his mother gently to her feet. In that moment, Rosalind warmed to him. Hitherto she had not been much attracted by the young man. But now there was a tenderness about him, which she had not thought possible. Obviously, he was at his best in his relationship with his mother.

Mrs Winter glanced up fleetingly at Rosalind.

"Thank you, my dear," she murmured, "you have been very kind."

Rosalind shook her head, unable to reply for the sudden lump in her throat. Yesterday, even this morning, when they met in the village, she would never have believed that she could ever feel such heart-tearing sympathy for Daphne Winter.

Giles led his mother out. The Colonel, still in his trance, stumbled after them. Rosalind went with them to their car, but no one spoke. She stood staring after them.

Someone spoke behind her and she jumped.

"Oh, I'm sorry," she gasped, "I was miles away."

It was Richard Seldon.

"I might as well go, too," he said, "nothing I can do here. I haven't seen or heard of Anne since she left years ago. I was at the hospital when you found her. You know my wife was taken ill last night. Didn't hear about all this until I got back to the factory."

Rosalind forced her mind away from Anne.

"How is Mrs Seldon?"

"Doing very well, thank you. She's never had a day's illness in her life before. She was sickening all the evening, then I had to call the doctor just after one. He thought she would be all right till the morning, but I had to call him again. At last, he sent for the ambulance and they took her to hospital. They operated at seven o'clock this morning. Of course, appendicitis is nothing these days, but it gave me a bit of a shock, I can tell you."

"I'm sure it did," murmured Rosalind politely, wondering if she would have to endure a description of the operation, cut by cut. Seldon seemed to be well launched on the topic.

"But my little bit of excitement is put in the shade by yours," he went on, with a half-smile. Rosalind realised that in an odd sort of fashion he was perfectly serious and more than a little put out by having the limelight snatched from him.

"I'm sure we would both have preferred to be left to our quiet lives," she replied.

"Naturally," he agreed, but she was disquieted by the expression in his eyes. She could have sworn that there was malice in them.

"Anne was Geoffrey's past, you might say," he added.

Rosalind was saved by David Kindersley. He came out of the front door at run.

"Oh, good, I've caught you, Richard," he said. "Can you give me a lift back to the factory? I came over with Geoffrey, but he will have to stay on here for a bit."

Seldon had no choice but agree. He moved over to his car and climbed into the driving seat.

David turned to Rosalind.

"Try not to brood over it," he advised her, "and do what you can for Geoffrey. He's got enough on his mind without adding this to it."

He was off before she could reply.

Rosalind turned back into the house. There was only Peter left now, and he would not linger. Bed was the only place for anyone with a cold like his. A wave of fatigue passed over her. She had already lived a century that day.

But there was still one more visitor to come. Ten minutes later, the doorbell rang.

"I'll go," said Geoffrey.

Thankfully, Rosalind let him.

He returned with Mrs Purvis.

"I'd heard," she said abruptly, "I had to come to find out if it is true. About Miss Anne?"

She was ignoring the two men, her attention fixed on Rosalind.

"Yes, Mrs Purvis. I'm afraid it is. She was under the tarpaulin on that pile of stuff out there."

Edna Purvis shrank visibly.

"How?"

Rosalind glanced quickly at Geoffrey for support. The whole thing was unbearable, not to be thought of.

"She was hit on the back of the head," Geoffrey said quietly, "it must have been very quick. The police think that she died instantaneously. There were no signs of a struggle. It is unlikely that she knew she was going to be struck, or even who struck her. She didn't have to suffer for any length of time."

Mrs Purvis gazed at him with hard eyes.

"How long was she there?"

"Not very long," Geoffrey went on, in that same gentle voice, "overnight, not more."

"Who did it?"

"That we don't know. The police will find out. It's the

more difficult because she has been away for so long. We don't know anything about her life over those years."

"You mean, someone followed her and killed her?"

Geoffrey shrugged.

"How else can it have happened?"

There was a short silence.

"Mrs Purvis," said Rosalind, at last, "you knew her quite well, didn't you?"

The woman's mouth tightened.

"Yes, I did. I worked up at the 'Hall' in those days."

Rosalind wanted to ask why Anne had gone away, what sort of person she was, why she should be the sort to drive anyone to murder. But while Geoffrey was there, she could not.

"It must be a great shock to you," she said lamely.

Mrs Purvis nodded.

"It needs a bit of getting used to," she admitted. "I'll be going now. Thank you for telling me. I'll be in in the morning, Mrs Lennard, if that's all right with you?"

"Of course it is, if you don't mind police all over the place. I expect they will be here tomorrow. But what about your mother-in-law? She's had a stroke, hasn't she?"

"Last night. They've taken her to the hospital in Broadgate, this morning."

Peter stood up.

"I can give you a lift into the village, if you like, Mrs Purvis," he offered, "I'm going that way."

She eyed him indifferently.

"Yes, I'd be glad of a lift, thank you very much."

"Well, be seeing you," Peter said. "Don't get up, Rosalind. We can see ourselves out."

Rosalind sank back on the settee and kicked off her shoes. Geoffrey, too, dropped wearily into a chair. Rosalind eyed him. They had things to talk about, and it was going to be tricky knowing where to begin.

It was better to plunge straight in.

"Why had she come back?"

"She wanted to make it up with her family."

At least he had not asked why she should expect him to know. So that was the first hurdle over.

"She had been away a long time?"

"Seventeen years."

"And she hadn't been in touch all that time?"

"No. As far as I know, none of us had heard from her until she rang me the night before last."

Relief flooded through Rosalind. He was going to tell her. And of his own accord, not because she had driven him into a corner from which he could not escape.

"She phoned you?" she asked, careful to keep her voice surprised.

Geoffrey smiled a small apologetic smile.

"I lied to you, darling. I told you it was David and he wanted me at the factory. But it was Anne, and she wanted to talk to me."

"But why didn't you tell me?"

"It was stupid of me. But it seemed the best at the time. I didn't want to do all the explaining. After all, Anne had gone out of my life so long ago. I should have told you, but I thought if I went into Broadgate to see her for a while, then that would be that."

"You were out a long time."

He frowned.

"I suppose I was. It all took so much longer than I had expected. And she was so much changed. I knew she would be older, but she was ill, too. I took her out to dinner, as if that would have helped her. But I suppose it made her feel a bit more welcome. She hadn't much time left for people to do her kindnesses, poor kid."

Rosalind felt the tears spring to her eyes.

"I'm glad you did that, Geoffrey. You couldn't know she was going to be murdered, but at least you can remember that you tried to help her."

But Geoffrey's face did not soften.

"I wasn't talking about that. In one way, that murder

was a kindness, too. Roz, she was dying of leukaemia. There is no cure and within a few months she would have been in a very bad way."

"Oh, no!" breathed Rosalind, appalled.

"Oh, yes," replied Geoffrey bitterly, "that's why she wanted to be reconciled with her family. Before the end. And her father wouldn't see her. He didn't believe me. I told him that she hadn't long and he wouldn't have it. He said it was just a trick to gain my sympathy."

"He hated her so much?"

"It was the old story. The fallen idol."

"Geoffrey, what happened? Why did she go away?"

He walked over to the window and stared out.

"There is no reason why you should not know. It will be common knowledge, soon, I imagine. Anne was eighteen, and she was engaged to me. A month before the wedding, her parents discovered that she was pregnant. I was not the father." He paused, then resumed. "She had the most appalling row with her mother and walked out. And that was the last we saw of her."

"But she was under age. Didn't anyone look for her?"

Geoffrey passed a hand over his face.

"David did. I was too angry to care. I don't know about her parents."

"David?"

"We were in our last year at the university, he and I. He used to spend a lot of time with us, in the vacations."

Rosalind did not press the matter. It seemed significant that it was David who had looked for the lost girl and not Geoffrey.

"Who was responsible?"

"We never knew. She wrote me a letter, before she went. She said she was sorry. She added that I must not look round for the father of her child. I didn't know him. I had the impression she was going away with him. But I could have been wrong. I must have been. When I saw her the other night, she said she had never married."

"What happened to the child?"

Geoffrey shook his head.

"I didn't like to ask. Perhaps she had it adopted. Or it might have died."

"It doesn't mean that she didn't keep in touch with the father. Was that what you were getting at, when you hinted to Mrs Purvis that the murderer followed her down here?"

For a moment, Geoffrey did not answer.

"No," he said, at last, "I was doing a bit of wishful thinking. I'm afraid it is not very likely."

"You mean, it was someone here, someone we know?"

"Yes. Roz, did you see the weapon?"

She shook her head.

"Do you know what it was?"

"The police said a spanner." She shied away from the thought.

"A spanner," he echoed, "a heavy spanner, with the ownership clearly stamped on the handle. Lennard Plastics. It came out of our vehicle repair shop."

CHAPTER 6

THEY heard it on the late news on Thursday. Scotland Yard had been called in on the Thanet murder. Murder Squad Superintendent Longton would start his investigations in Broadgate in the morning.

"They will come here first," Geoffrey prophesied. "Do you want me to stay at home?"

Rosalind shook her head.

"No, it will be all right. They can't eat me, and there is very little that I can tell them."

Geoffrey went off to the factory, vaguely dissatisfied. Rosalind, telling herself that it was thoughtful of him to offer to stay with her when he was so busy at work, was left wondering why he should want to be on the spot when the London detectives arrived. It set up a nasty little doubt in her mind that Anne's murder had upset him more than she realised. Perhaps the old love had never really died. Sickly, she put the thought from her, ashamed at the sudden surge of jealousy which shot through her.

Mrs Purvis arrived at her usual time, and set to, in the house, as if nothing had happened. Rosalind, who found that she herself could settle to nothing, marvelled at her.

"How is your mother-in-law?" she asked, to start any topic of conversation which would keep her own thoughts occupied.

"Well enough. No worse and no better. But it's her second stroke, and she is in a bad way. But she is putting up a fight. She's paralysed all down one side. We had a terrible time with her till they came and took her away. Up nearly all night, we was."

Rosalind made sympathetic noises.

"And to think," said Mrs Purvis suddenly, "that Miss Anne must have gone past my door while I was sitting up with the old woman, and I never knew it."

Rosalind stared at her. Of course, it must have happened. She had not thought how Anne Winter had reached their garden that night, but she must have come through the village, and past Mrs Purvis's cottage.

"You were fond of her, weren't you?"

Edna Purvis hesitated. She was not the sort of woman to wear her heart on her sleeve, or to advertise her feelings. But Anne was dead, and the grief weighed heavily on her. There was no one at home who would understand.

"Yes," she admitted, "I loved her as if she were my own child. If she had come to me, when she found she was in trouble, I would have thought of something. I often used to wonder how she managed."

"She didn't go away with the man, then?"

Mrs Purvis glanced at her sharply.

"Whatever gave you that idea?"

They were interrupted. A car was turning into the drive, and voices were raised outside. Rosalind, expecting the police, ran to the front door.

It was Glenda, and she was arguing with the young policeman on guard over the place where Anne had been found.

"Oh, Rosalind!" she exclaimed thankfully, "do tell this young man that I'm a relative. He won't let me come in."

The constable, torn between his orders and the devastating loveliness of Glenda Hardwick, blushed furiously.

Rosalind walked over to them.

"This is my sister-in-law, constable. Why can't she come in?"

"The Inspector said no one was to come in, until the Superintendent from Scotland Yard had had a look round. He doesn't want the ground disturbed."

"But that's ridiculous," Glenda broke in. "I'm sure there were dozens of cars over it yesterday. And the lane is too narrow for parking."

"That's true enough," agreed Rosalind, although she wished that she dared take refuge behind the instructions of the Law, and turn Glenda away.

"My inspector," began the man, but Rosalind cut him short.

"I realise you have your instructions," she smiled, "but Mrs Hardwick won't be staying long. Couldn't she just leave the car where it is? She can always move it if the Superintendent arrives before she leaves."

The constable hesitated. He would like to oblige the ladies, but his inspector was a hard man, and the Murder Squad people would surely be more so.

"She has only come to collect a shopping list for me," Rosalind went on with sudden inspiration, "she won't be above ten minutes."

"Oh, well, in that case, it's all right, madam."

Glenda pouted. It wasn't what she had in mind at all,

but it would have to do. She followed Rosalind into the house.

"I came to see if there is anything I could do," she announced.

"Thanks, but I can manage, Glenda. Your mother kept Sally with her last night, much to my relief. I can't see that the police will be around here after today. Then the builders can take the rest of their stuff away, and we can be peaceful again."

"I shouldn't count on it," retorted Glenda, "they will be asking questions. Everyone who knew Anne will be in for it."

"You mean Geoffrey? He has already told them everything he knows."

"Has he?" said Glenda.

Rosalind drew her breath in sharply. She didn't care for Glenda's tone, but she was not prepared to start an argument.

"You knew her, too," she reminded her.

Glenda shrugged.

"I was only a child. I remember her vaguely, that's all."

The temptation was too great for Rosalind.

"What was she like?"

"Anne? She was all right. We lived in St Mark's then, only a couple of miles away from here. She used to spend a lot of time at our house. She used to play with me. Why?"

"Oh, I'm interested, that's all," replied Rosalind vaguely, "I was there when they found her."

"What did she look like?" asked Glenda avidly. This was the sort of thing she had come to hear.

"As if she was asleep, only her eyes were open," said Rosalind slowly, facing the memory squarely, "she looked peaceful."

She suddenly felt better, remembering exactly what she had seen, shorn of the things which her imagination had added. She had seen neither blood, nor wound, nor the weapon lying beside the dead woman. Only a figure lying in a natural pose, like a deep sleeper. She had the grace to be grateful to Glenda for making her face it.

"I wondered what sort of a person she was," Rosalind went on.

"We all like to know our rivals," observed Glenda with unconcealed malice.

Rosalind kept her face straight.

"Rivals?"

Glenda laughed.

"Geoffrey's the faithful sort. One woman only, and all that. Not that you need worry now. Anne's dead."

Rosalind's hands itched to take her glamorous relative by the shoulders and shake her till her teeth rattled. Something of it must have shown on her face, for Glenda added hastily,

"I'd better run now, or that nice policeman out there will be getting worried. Do you want me to do any shopping for you?"

"No, thank you," said Rosalind stonily.

"Well, that's up to you. Let me know if I can do anything. And try not to worry about Geoffrey. I'm sure it will all work out."

Rosalind found it cold comfort. She was glad to see Glenda leave, before her temper got the better of her. She wondered what she had done, to arouse so much spite in Geoffrey's sister.

Her thoughts turned back to Anne Winter. Rosalind wished that she had known her, in life; that she had had an opportunity to applaud her courage, to tell her she was doing the right thing. She could imagine how Anne had felt over the years, cut off from her family, earning her living in a cold world. Rosalind herself knew all about that, and she had a child to support, too. And then, when Anne knew the end was approaching, and wanting to die in peace, seek out her family, swallow her pride and come home. Rosalind wondered if under similar circumstances she would ever have—might ever have in some black future—the courage to do the same thing.

She was still thinking about it when the Scotland Yard detective arrived. She heard a car stop in the drive, and then the voices. This time, she did not rush to the front door. Instead, she sat in the drawing room waiting. They would reach her soon enough. From upstairs came the sounds of Mrs Purvis busily running the vacuum cleaner over the bedrooms. And out in the garden, a bird sang. The sun was out and the day beginning to heat up. A few miles away, on the sands at Broadgate, the crowds of holidaymakers would be massed. . . .

The doorbell rang.

Mrs Purvis switched off the cleaner, but Rosalind was already in the hall, calling that she would answer it.

There were two men standing in the porch. One was of middle height, with sharp, lined features. A ferret in a grey suit and felt hat.

"Mrs Lennard? I'm Superintendent Longton," he was saying.

Rosalind scarcely heard him. She was staring at his companion.

He was a large man, in his early thirties, with thick black hair. He, too, was dressed in a suit of muted tweed.

"Good God!" he said blankly.

Superintendent Longton turned on him.

"What's the matter, Thornley? Do you know this lady?"

Detective Sergeant Barry Thornley cleared his throat. A deep blush rose over his neck and face.

"She's my sister, sir."

*   *   *

"Why didn't you tell me?" demanded the Superintendent.

Barry Thornley calmly finished his mouthful of food before attempting an answer. The two men had returned for lunch to the "Cross Keys" in Parrington village, where they were putting up. For the rest of the morning since the surprise recognition of Rosalind Lennard, Longton had made neither comment nor reference to it. Now, it had come. The Superintendent was regarding his sergeant with an unkind eye.

Barry had worked with him often enough to know that his bark was worse than his bite.

"I didn't know," he said. "I haven't seen my sister for nearly twelve years."

Longton grunted.

"Since she was seventeen, in fact?"

Barry nodded.

"She insisted on marrying a chap none of us liked. She was under age, and my parents refused permission, so she went to the magistrates. She managed to convince them all right. There was a fearful row, she left home and that was the last we saw of her."

"What had you got against Lennard?"

"Lennard? It wasn't Lennard she was marrying. It was a bloke called Dick Johnson. He was twenty-two and he had quite a decent post in the Civil Service. Good-looking fellow, too, and bags of charm. He had the the magistrates eating out of his hand. But he was a twerp all right. He and I went to the same school. He was a couple of years ahead of me, but I knew all about him. Not that there was anything I could make a definite charge about, but I knew he would never make her happy. I'm damned glad to know that she has managed to ditch him. She looks as though she has done pretty well for herself in her second."

Longton's eyebrows rose, but he said nothing.

"I hope," added Barry.

The thought lay between them : if he doesn't turn out to be a murderer.

"Do you want to be taken off it?" asked Longton. "They could send someone else down."

Barry shook his head.

"On the whole, I'd rather not, at the moment, if you don't mind, sir. I'd like to have a talk with Rosalind and see how she feels about it. There is no need for anyone to know that we are related, and if by any chance her husband is involved, I would rather be there to gather up the bits."

Superintendent Longton nodded gloomily.

"Some women have a genius for picking bad ones," he remarked. He looked at his watch. "You can go and see her now. Be back in half an hour."

Rosalind said, "I thought you would be coming."

Barry stepped into the hall for the second time that day. He looked round appreciatively.

"Nice place," he commented.

"Yes," she replied and told him more by that one word than if she had let out a torrent.

"You're happy?"

She nodded.

"Now. I married Geoffrey just over four months ago."

"What happened to Dick?"

She turned away.

"He died."

"I'm sorry."

Rosalind sighed.

"I'm sorry he had to go the way he did. He was drowned. We were on holiday in Cornwall. He would insist on swimming, when he had been warned not to. Two men risked their lives trying to save him. Fortunately they survived."

The bitterness in her tone cut at Barry.

"Just the sort of damnfool thing he would do," he said; "he never had the smallest consideration for other people."

She swung round to face him.

"I don't think I could have borne it if those men had died, too. I'll never forget standing on the cliffs and watching them—and Dick. Their wives were by me and one of them was sobbing and the other was standing there, frozen. They struggled back to the beach with him, but it was no good. All I could think of was relief that it was all over and they were safe. The two men, I mean. I knew there was no hope for Dick. And—God forgive me—that was a relief, too."

Barry put his arm round his sister's shoulders and shook her gently.

"Roz," he said, "snap out of it. You didn't ask him to go swimming, did you?"

"I begged him not to."

"Then stop blaming yourself. You are, aren't you?"

She looked up at him. The years rolled away and it was as if they were still teenagers.

"I've always felt that I should have been more sorry. Oh, I was sorry he had lost his life, but I couldn't pretend that I wasn't glad to be free of him."

"When did it happen?"

"Six years ago. How time passes. Sally was only four."

"Sally?"

Rosalind laughed.

"Of course, you don't know. You're an uncle, Barry."

"Where is she now?"

"At school in Broadgate. She has been staying with Geoffrey's mother for a couple of nights, thank goodness, but she will be home tonight. If your people will let the builders take that heap of stuff away. I don't want her home until that has gone."

But Barry wasn't listening.

"Roz," he burst out, "you had six years on your own. How did Dick leave you? For money, I mean."

"Very badly. He hadn't saved anything, and he thought he would live for ever. There were no insurances. We lived in a rented flat, too."

"What did you live on?"

She smiled.

"We managed very well. I brushed up my shorthand and typing, and I got a good job."

"Why didn't you come home?"

"I was too proud," Rosalind admitted. "You all tried to stop me from marrying Dick and I wouldn't listen to you and of course you were all right. He wasn't any good as a husband. He never took to being married, not even after Sally arrived."

Barry could have pointed out to her that there were two sides to the question. His mother still kept Rosalind's photograph in the lounge, and had never stopped regretting that she had allowed herself to be separated from her daughter. But even now, Rosalind must come back of her own accord.

"I've been thinking a lot about making contact again," she was saying, as if in answer to his thoughts, "I didn't know if I would be welcome."

"You can take it that you would be," he replied gravely, not daring to appear too eager, but he was thinking about the phone call which he would make that evening, and the joy that it would bring.

"It was Anne, of course," she said. "Anne Winter. She made me think. She was like me, Barry, cut off from her family. She came back to make it up with them, and she never got the chance. They will have to live with that for the rest of their lives. They are bound to regret every-thing—so much."

It jerked him back to the present situation.

"Look, Roz, this is a thing we have to discuss."

"Yes, of course. I was forgetting. You've come on in the world, Barry. You were pounding a beat when I—left."

"The point is, we don't normally expect police officers to investigate things which might concern members of their own families. The Superintendent has offered to let me go back to London and get another assistant down here."

"But I'm not involved," objected Rosalind. "I didn't know Anne."

"Your husband did."

"Yes, but that was all a long time ago. If you have any choice, I would much rather you stayed, Barry."

"So would I, to be truthful. But, look Roz, don't broadcast it that I'm your brother."

Her face changed.

"Oh!"

Barry grabbed her again, and this time, shook her quite roughly.

"I didn't mean it that way, idiot," he said furiously. "It's only that if it became common knowledge, some officious busybody might insist on my being taken off the case. Now do you understand?"

Rosalind hung her head.

"I'm sorry. I was stupid."

"You were. You can tell Geoffrey, and swear him to secrecy. Now I must go. The Super is waiting for me. I'll be back when I can."

Rosalind saw him to the door.

"I do hope you find out soon who killed her. I feel so sorry for her. I'm sure we should have had a lot in common, she and I. I wish I had known her. She had such a nice voice."

Barry swung round.

"What did you say?"

Rosalind stared at him, surprised.

"She had such a nice voice."

"I thought you never met her."

"I didn't. It was over the phone. The first time she rang up, I took the call. Geoffrey was out."

"You didn't mention this before."

"I never thought about it. Is it important?"

"Anything to do with Anne Winter could be important. What did you say to her?"

Rosalind shrugged.

"Nothing much. Just that Geoffrey wasn't in and could I take a message."

"Did she leave one?"

"No," Rosalind was suddenly filled with uneasiness, "she hung up on me."

"Did she know who you were?"

Rosalind's face cleared. The explanation was quite simple.

"It came as a bit of a surprise to her, I think. She couldn't have known about me, though she might have guessed that Geoffrey would have married. I suppose it was a bit of a jolt, all the same. She couldn't have explained herself to me."

Detective Sergeant Barry Thornley gazed at his sister with compassion. He didn't like the sound of that at all.

CHAPTER 7

STANLEY THREADWELL nodded his head in agreement.

"That suits me, Lennard. Monday morning at eleven o'clock. But I hope you are not labouring under the impression that getting the meeting over will leave you free to attend to your private affairs. You will have an extraordinary general meeting to organise."

"I am not in the habit of letting my private affairs interfere with business," replied Geoffrey stiffly, "and while I agree that this matter will have to be explained to the shareholders, I feel that it should wait until the normal annual general meeting. By that time, the position will be clearer, we shall be able to tell them what action we have taken, and I hope that we shall also have found the culprit."

Threadwell snorted.

"The way you're going on, you'll never catch him in a million years."

"And what do you suggest that we do?"

The other shrugged and rose to his feet.

"I'd find him. Or her, as the case may be."

"Her?" queried Geoffrey.

"Her," repeated Threadwell softly, "you want to get to know your staff, Lennard."

Geoffrey stood up.

"Will you please explain yourself?"

But Threadwell was already half-way to the door.

"Do your own snooping," he recommended.

In a few strides, Geoffrey crossed the office to stand between Threadwell and the door to Miss Summers' room.

"Are you hinting that you know something about one of my staff that I don't?"

"I'm not one to spread gossip," said Threadwell virtuously.

"If it has any bearing on this business, it is your duty as one of the directors to tell me," retorted Geoffrey.

"So that you can claim all the credit for uncovering the culprit," sneered Threadwell, and made to push past him.

Geoffrey flung open the door between the two offices.

It was pointless arguing with Threadwell. He was not going to let out what information he possessed. That was to be kept to make trouble for Geoffrey in front of the shareholders. It might not even be true, but the innuendo would be enough.

Peter Maynard was sitting on a corner of Miss Summers' desk. He was talking to a tall, slim blonde. Of Miss Summers herself, there was no sign.

Threadwell followed Geoffrey into the room.

"Lucille," he barked, "keep away from him. You'll catch his cold too."

Lucille Threadwell laughed.

"I was out with him in the boat when we got that wetting," she reminded her father. "I didn't catch cold."

"Because I insisted that you had a hot bath and went to bed the moment you came in," he retorted. "If you want to live a long time, you've got to look after yourself."

"I'd rather have a short life and a merry one," said Lucille flippantly.

Threadwell glared at her.

"You'll learn," he prophesied grimly. He turned to Peter, "And as for you, young man, you ought to be in bed. We want you fit for the board meeting on Monday."

Peter started to agree, but was overtaken by a sneeze.

"You see," said Threadwell, "he ought to be at home, Lennard."

Geoffrey shrugged.

"That's up to Peter."

"It would suit your book very nicely for him to be out of action on Monday, wouldn't it? One vote less. No wonder you wanted to fix that meeting so quickly. You knew Peter had come back to work too soon. You could safely send him home again on Monday morning, pretending that he wasn't fit." He glanced balefully from Geoffrey to his cousin : "It wouldn't surprise me if you hadn't fixed it up between you. If I thought that, Peter, I'd make damned sure you never laid eyes on Lucille again," he boiled up suddenly.

Lucille laid her hand on his arm.

"Daddy, don't work yourself up. Of course Peter will be there on Monday. And his cold will be better. Simpson can take him home now. He can go to bed and stay there until Monday morning. I'll give Mrs Jones a ring. She can take him his food and make sure he stays indoors. And please don't imagine that Peter caught this cold deliberately so that he could duck out of the board meeting. You know that's nonsense. You can't catch colds like that. Now, you come along with me. You said you wanted to see Mr Hardwick, so you go to his office, while I tell Simpson to bring the car round for Peter."

Threadwell went with her without a word. At the door, Lucille turned. She winked at Geoffrey and blew a kiss to Peter.

Geoffrey grinned.

"She certainly knows how to handle the old devil," he said, when the door was safely shut behind them.

"You had better go home, now, Peter. Today's Friday. You've two clear days. But you will have to be here on Monday."

"You know what will happen, don't you, Geoffrey?" Peter said thoughtfully, "I shall have to vote for him."

Geoffrey took a turn round the room.

"I'm sorry this decision is being forced on you, Peter."

"He's made it quite clear that if I don't do as he says, I can say goodbye to Lucille."

"I know it is difficult for you. But you came in with us almost from the beginning. There were so few of us then. Just you, me, David, Elsie Summers and a couple of men. It was damned hard work, too, but we enjoyed it. I never thought we should grow so big. A lot of that has been due to you, Peter. And I never thought we should come to this sort of fix, either."

Peter could not meet his eyes.

"It's no good, Geoffrey. I can't give up Lucille."

"Won't she defy her father? Doesn't anyone ever gainsay him? She seems to manage him well enough."

"Not over this. He'll cut her off. She'd be unhappy, Geoffrey. Oh, I know I earn plenty, but I couldn't give her what she is used to. She doesn't know anything about money. It's just something that's there, in unlimited supply, to be used. She would ruin me in a year. I know it sounds mean, Geoffrey, but I just can't afford to offend Threadwell. And he knows it."

Geoffrey turned away.

"It's your decision, Peter. Now, for heaven's sake, go home, or I shall have that man in my hair all day, demanding that you do. And be in on Monday."

Geoffrey did not return to his own office. He went out of the building, over to David's place. There, at least, was someone on whom he could rely. One of the original ones. . . .

Like Peter. . . .

It hurt, there was no blinking the fact. He had known for days that there was a likelihood that Peter would desert him. But to hear it from his cousin's own lips. . . .

Suddenly, he was remembering all the years of their youth. Peter, five years his junior, had lost his parents very young. It had been Geoffrey's mother who had taken him in, although her husband was in his last, lingering illness. And Peter had stayed on with them when she remarried. He was like a younger brother to Geoffrey. Peter, he thought sadly, was always self-centred. Perhaps it was due to being left an orphan and a penniless one at that.

David was not in his office. With an exclamation of annoyance, Geoffrey turned away.

While he was here, he might as well have a word with Seldon. There were things which had to be said between them.

Richard Seldon was in. He was sitting glumly at his desk, skimming through a file.

"Richard," said Geoffrey briskly, "the board meeting is at eleven on Monday. O.K. ?"

Seldon nodded. "Suits me."

"Threadwell is pressing for an extraordinary general meeting of the shareholders. He intends to force a vote on Monday."

Seldon removed his pipe from its permanent position at the corner of his mouth.

"I know. I agree with him."

"I thought you might."

"I've every right to," said Seldon, ruffled at Geoffrey's tone. "You've only yourself to thank. You won't listen to a word of advice from an older man. But it's all of a

c

piece. You younger men think you know everything. But you're an irresponsible lot. No sense of property or respect of other people's feelings."

Geoffrey ignored that.

"What you mean is, you'll vote with Threadwell, on Monday. And I suppose," he added, tired of all the hedging and wanting to have it all out in the open, "if he succeeds in carrying the motion, you will also vote against my re-election at the shareholders' meeting? And get yourself voted in?"

Seldon smirked.

"I've a lot of experience. If the shareholders want me, there is no reason why I shouldn't be elected in your place."

"You flatter yourself."

"I was running a company before you were born."

"And where to? You were damn near bankrupt when we bought you out."

Seldon's face drained of colour.

"Trust you to throw that in my face, Geoffrey Lennard. I've always known that you would, one day. But don't think I'll forget it. Or forgive it. And you'll regret it. Mark my words, you'll regret it."

Geoffrey slammed out of the office, furious with himself for being goaded into losing his temper, furious with Seldon for his self-satisfied readiness to wreck everything they had built, furious with Threadwell for bringing all this down on them. He had never felt more helpless in his life. He had built all this up, he and David, and Peter, too. Bitterly, he could see that the cards were stacked against him. He would lose it all.

Elsie Summers was back at her desk when he reached her office. She took one glance at his face.

"Geoffrey, what is the matter?"

"Seldon," he said shortly.

"Oh, him," she said contemptuously, "don't take any notice of him. He's got a bee in his bonnet this morning.

He's nattering on about the irresponsibility of the younger generation. I don't know what it's all about. I didn't stop to listen."

"He mentioned that to me, too. I don't suppose it is anything important. He's such a fusser. No, it's that meeting on Monday. Look, Threadwell has Peter and Seldon. I can rely on David and Edward."

Miss Summers said nothing. She did not like Edward Hardwick. She never had, not from the moment that he had joined the firm, some eight years previously. And he and Threadwell seemed to have a lot to say to each other these days. She hoped that Geoffrey was not nursing false hopes.

"So it boils down to the Colonel," Geoffrey was saying. "I don't know which way he will vote. It could be either way, and if Threadwell has promised him some special post for Giles, that could do the trick."

"He must know that Giles can't do much," she protested.

"He is still his father and he would like to see him properly settled. But the Colonel is fair. He won't let me be jockeyed out of control unless he is convinced that I am inefficient. There is one thing which I can do which might sway him on to my side, and would rob Threadwell of a bit of his ammunition for the shareholders. And that is find the source of the information leak. Find the traitor, in fact. And I have two days."

Miss Summers stared at him.

"What can you hope to find out in two days? We've been investigating it for weeks and have come up with nothing."

"Threadwell is hinting that he knows who is responsible. What he can find out, we can. Elsie, which woman member of our staff who had access to those drawings has also got light fingers?"

Miss Summers clung on to the edge of her desk. She wondered, in despair, if her face was giving her away.

CHAPTER 8

SUPERINTENDENT LONGTON surveyed the classical front of Parrington Hall. It was a gracious house, with a neat pillared doorway, flanked by four long windows on either side. It rose to three storeys, above them a shallow roof and solid chimneys.

"Nice place," he commented, taking in the carefully tended drive and garden, the house paint which showed no chips or cracks. "Must cost a packet to keep up. No wonder the Colonel works for his living."

He stumped up the steps and rang the doorbell.

Barry Thornley hung back. His mind wasn't on his job. He was worrying about his sister. He came to when a uniformed maid opened the door.

They were taken into the Colonel's study, at the back of the house, overlooking a large garden as neat and tidy as the rest of the property. The buzz of an unseen motor mower cut through the still heat of early summer.

Colonel Winter, who had been standing gazing out of the window, turned to greet them. Barry registered him as a fine figure of a man, almost the stock story-book idea of a soldier, until you saw the eyes. This was no unimaginative Blimp.

Longton mumbled introductions.

"About your daughter, sir."

The Colonel gave them chairs, and settled himself behind his desk. He tidied a pen tray already arranged with military precision.

"When did you last see her?"

The haunted eyes were veiled by their lids.

"Over seventeen years ago," the Colonel replied in his brisk clipped voice.

"Not since? But she had written?"

"No. There had been no contact between her and her

family since she left. Superintendent, my daughter disgraced herself and us. She went away. It was better."

He might have been an untalented actor reading a part. Barry wondered if the Colonel saw himself as a bluff military man, and spoke his lines accordingly. But the important thing was the soul inside.

"But she did come back," Longton was saying.

"Yes. I did not see her."

"But you knew she was back?"

"Mr Lennard told me Anne had approached him."

"And what was your reaction, sir?"

For a moment it seemed that man's control might slip. There was an almost visual battle between the real suffering man, and the imposed image.

"I informed Mr Lennard that I wished to have nothing to do with her," he replied at last, and with a great effort. "As far as I am concerned, I had no daughter."

"Why do you suppose she came back?" Longton pressed him.

On the smooth leather top of the desk, the Colonel's hands closed into tight fists.

"I have no idea."

"And all this happened on the day she was killed," said Longton heavily. "She comes back, for the first time in many years, you reject her and she is murdered," he added, with deliberate provocation.

Colonel Winter clamped his lips together and did not answer. Superintendent Longton nodded, well satisfied.

Crafty old devil, thought Barry. A remark like that would produce an outburst from any normal bereaved father. So the Colonel is hiding something, is he? He's a hope! Longton will winkle it out.

"Do you know where she has been living?"

"No, Superintendent, I do not. I told you, there has been no contact."

"Her handbag was beside the body. There is a letter addressed to her at a London address."

"A letter?"

Longton smiled cynically over the Colonel's pathetic eagerness. No doubt everyone would be relieved to think that the murder was the work of some outsider, but the spanner ruled that out.

"A business letter," he said gently, "about dry-cleaning or something. It's only important for the address."

Colonel Winter turned his head away.

"I see," he said quietly.

"So far we haven't traced your daughter's movements," Longton went on briskly, "nor have I studied the report from the pathologist, yet, but it is clear that she was killed on Wednesday night, latish. Where were you, sir, that evening?"

The Colonel jerked to attention, his armour penetrated at last.

"No!" he exclaimed.

"Oh, yes, you could have done it, sir," replied Longton, understanding him. "Fathers have killed daughters before now. And I shall be asking everyone who knew her, and everyone who could have obtained that weapon, for accounts of their movements on Wednesday night. Which includes you."

The Colonel seemed to shrink in his chair.

"I was here, all evening," he said dully.

"There were people who can corroborate that?"

"Yes, of course. The servants. No, I think they were out. I don't really know."

"Your wife? Or your son?"

But the Colonel was busy thinking about something else.

"You'll have to ask them," he said vaguely.

"I shall," Longton promised him grimly. "In fact, I should like to see the rest of the household now, if they are all here."

"Yes, certainly, Superintendent," he replied, reaching over to press the bell beside the fireplace.

Longton stood up.

"And I shall want to talk to you again, sir. I advise you to tell me everything you know about your daughter. You want her murderer brought to justice, don't you?"

But the Colonel was too preoccupied with his own thoughts to do more than nod perfunctorily.

The maid took them to Mrs Winter's sitting room. This was a beautiful room, luxuriously furnished. It might have been an illustration from a glossy magazine, and with about as much character.

Mrs Winter was elegant in black. She went through the motions of being a sophisticated hostess, but there was a tremor in her hands which she could not conceal.

No, she did not know that her daughter had re-appeared. Her husband had not told her.

"It was my Women's Institute evening, Superintendent. I would never have gone if I had thought Anne was back. My husband should have told me. I thought he was a bit strange that evening, but naturally with all the trouble over the board meeting, I assumed it was that."

"Trouble?" queried Longton brightly.

"It's no good asking me about it," she said hastily, "I don't understand these things. But my husband was worrying about it. He had to choose between that Mr Threadwell and Geoffrey. It wasn't easy because he has always thought so highly of Geoffrey. That's why he put money into the company when Geoffrey wanted to expand. It was years ago, of course, while he was still in the Army. Then, when he retired, he went into the business. He and Geoffrey have always got on so well, but there was that leak, it's all such a pity. It's difficult for my husband, too, because I think he feels we owe Geoffrey something—because of Anne, you know—and he has such a sense of the family honour."

Longton, Barry noted, was wearing his cat-with-canary smile. Mrs Winter might not understand business affairs, but at least she was willing to *talk*.

"I want to know about Anne," he interrupted.

"Oh, yes. They were engaged. Geoffrey and Anne. So suitable, we all thought. The Lennards are a good family, though no one has as much money nowadays as they did, do they? But we all knew that Geoffrey would make his way in the world. They used to live at St Mark's. That's the next village. We've known them all our lives. Geoffrey couldn't afford to keep up their place, so he sold up and started the factory with the proceeds. The old house is a convalescent home now. Geoffrey's mother was glad to leave it, I think. It was," she added, glancing round with satisfaction at the elegant Georgian room, "quite hideously Victorian and madly inconvenient."

Longton was listening patiently. He liked this sort of witness. You never quite knew what would emerge from the ragbag of their minds.

"But the engagement was broken off?" he prompted.

Mrs Winter sighed.

"Of course, it had to be. No one could expect Geoffrey . . ." she tailed off.

"What happened? Why did your daughter leave home?"

"Must we? It's all so long ago."

"She's dead. I must know about her."

"All right," she said reluctantly, "she was going to have a baby. She wouldn't tell me who was the father. I had to deal with it all on my own. My husband was serving with his regiment. He was in the Far East. Of course, he came home, but by then it was all over. Anne had gone. It hurt him terribly. He was so fond of her."

"Do you know where she went?"

Mrs Winter shook her head.

"I didn't know what to do."

"Did you look for her?"

"My husband said she had made her choice and that was that."

"And you never heard from her?"

"No."

"Did you never wonder what had become of her?"

Mrs Winter's eyes suddenly brimmed over with tears.

"Of course I wondered. But you get used to things. And Anne was always secretive. She wasn't an ideal daughter. She would never tell me things. Just as she wouldn't confide in me when she was in a real mess. She wasn't fair to me. Nor to her little brother. There was ten years between them, and she never took to him. And now to come back like this. So typical of her. She was a very thoughtless girl."

Superintendent Longton regarded his witness with appreciation.

"And what about Mr Geoffrey Lennard? How did he take the breaking of his engagement and the reason for it?"

"He was terribly angry and hurt. He was in his last year at the university. He threw himself into his work, I suppose. He did quite brilliantly, I believe. He went away for a couple of years, then came back to start up the factory. But he must have been far more in love with Anne than she deserved," she added with sudden irritation, "for he kept her photograph on his desk for years. And he never so much as looked at a woman. Not until he met Rosalind."

Barry looked up at that. But he kept silence.

"It would be a bit of a shock to him, to have Anne reappear, just when he had married someone else?" Longton suggested quietly.

Mrs Winter nodded.

"It must have been. Poor Geoffrey! I often wondered," she added, after a slight pause, "if it might not have been he. . . . But that wouldn't have made sense," she finished briskly. "I mean there would have been no reason why the engagement should have been broken, would there?"

Barry was surprised that Longton let it pass, but knew better than venture a comment.

"One thing more, Mrs Winter," he said mildly. "On Wednesday night, were the servants here?"

"We have only two living in now. The cook and the maid. The charwoman comes daily and finishes at five. They have Wednesday night off. As it is my W.I. night, we never entertain then. They usually go into Broadgate, to the cinema or a dance, I suppose. They come back on the last bus, half past ten from Broadgate, a quarter past eleven here."

"And what time did you return from the Women's Institute?"

She stared at him stupidly.

"I can't see why you want to know that. We finish at nine, but we had an extra meeting afterwards, this week. There was rather an argument and it dragged on and on. It must have been ten-thirty before I reached home."

"And was your husband here then?"

This time, she stared with comprehension.

"Of course," she said coldly, but her voice shook.

Longton nodded.

"That's all—for the moment—Mrs Winter. I'll just have a word with your son."

"Giles?" she cut in and the fear in her voice was unmistakable. "He can't tell you anything about Anne. He was only a child when she left."

"He was here on Wednesday."

"But he couldn't have had anything to do with it. He wouldn't have known her if he had met her face to face in the street."

Giles himself showed none of his mother's panic.

"Did I know she was back?" he said. "Yes, Superintendent, I did. All of us knew, at the works. Geoffrey told David and Peter, and of course the word got round."

"Didn't you want to see your sister?" asked Longton.

"Why should I?" countered Giles. "I could hardly remember her. She meant nothing to me. She made herself cheap and she went away, and good riddance to her. Why she wanted to come back is beyond me."

Longton eyed him with disfavour.

"And where were you on Wednesday evening?"

Giles laughed.

"You can't catch me, Superintendent. I've an alibi. I was in Broadgate with a couple of friends. You can have their names. We were prowling round the dance halls, seeing what talent was available. We rolled home at midnight. Good enough?"

"Sergeant Thornley will have those names and addresses, please," replied Longton repressively.

Ten minutes later, they were driving back in the direction of Broadgate.

"This is where we split up for a while, Sergeant. You go to that hotel she was staying it. See what you can find there. See if you can find out how she got to Parrington on Wednesday night. She might have been on that bus. Or try the taxis. She wouldn't have walked."

"By car?" suggested Barry.

"If it was, it must have been the murderer's. So we will check all those cars at the factory. There might be a trace in one of them. You can drop me there. I want to talk to all those people."

They drove on in silence for a while.

"That Mrs Winter," said Longton suddenly, when they were nearly at the factory gates, "isn't nearly as silly as she would have us think. She's got a nasty idea under her hat, and she would throw anyone to the wolves to protect her son. Or her husband. Or both. Look at the way she was laying for Geoffrey Lennard."

"The Colonel," said Barry carefully, not wanting at this stage to discuss his brother-in-law with the Superintendent, "is an odd sort of man."

"Fanatic for tidiness," agreed Longton. "He might have tidied an inconvenient daughter away, at that."

CHAPTER 9

THE "Cross Keys", the only pub in Parrington which let rooms, was not one of the finest English hostelries. The house was old, but not picturesque; the furniture and cooking no more than adequate.

Superintendent Marsh, of the county police, apologised for it. There was, he explained, more luxurious accommodation in Broadgate, but since it was the end of May and a heatwave, the place was already nearly full up with summer visitors.

Longton waved the apology aside.

"Can't stand holiday crowds, mooning around and getting in the way of folks with a job of work to do," he declared, forgetful of the short time each year that he was thankful to devote to the same pursuit, "and I hope that we shan't be here long," he added, flinging a bulging brief-case down on his bed. "I'll go through that little lot and then see where we are."

Marsh grinned and left him to it.

Longton sighed, took off his jacket, settled himself in the only comfortable chair in the room, and began to read steadily through the papers from the brief-case.

Half an hour later, there was a brief knock on the door and Barry Thornley peered in.

"Oh, there you are," said Longton, disagreeably, crossed by the stifling atmosphere of the little room and the confusion of the beginning of a new case.

Barry took no notice. He, too, was sticky with heat, and longing for a beer. But opening time was still half an hour away, and there was work to be done.

"Well?" demanded Longton.

Barry perched himself on the windowsill.

"That hotel she was staying at," he began, " 'The Ship'. It's down by the jetty. It's a little place, used chiefly by commercials. Not the sort of place to attract the holidaymakers. Quiet, and, from the smell of the kitchen, nothing more adventurous than ham and eggs ever served there. But the woman who runs it is bright enough. Anyway, she had interested herself a bit in Anne Winter. She thought she looked ill. And it wasn't the first time she'd been there."

Longton looked up.

"What's that?"

"It was Winter's second visit. She was here in January. From the fourth to the sixth."

"Well. Go on."

"This woman, Mrs Pardoe, can't remember much about the first visit. Winter was there just for those few days, she spent most of her time out, but Mrs P. doesn't know where. And as far as she can remember, she had no visitors. Not the first time she was here, that is."

"But she did on the second?"

"Yes. Winter arrived on Tuesday morning. She had telephoned the night before, for a reservation. She had her lunch at 'The Ship', then she went out for the rest of the day, not returning until after eleven p.m. Wednesday, she was out in the morning, back for lunch, then she stayed in her room all afternoon. There were two phone calls for her. Mrs Pardoe can't remember the times of them, unfortunately, but she does know they were both after four o'clock, and on each occasion it was a man's voice. What she can't say is, if it was the same person both times, or two different men."

Longton nodded.

"Yes. Go on."

"At about six o'clock, Winter came down, handed in her key and went out. And that was the last that Mrs Pardoe saw of her. Now we come to the sticky part. Mrs P. then went out for the evening, leaving the place in the charge of a young woman who might be the original Dumb Blonde. I wouldn't leave her in charge of a chained bicycle, but that's Mrs P.'s business. The point is, a man called to see Anne Winter, and when he found she was out, went away and came back again later. But that is as much as the Dumb Blonde can tell us. She has no idea of the times that he called, nor can she describe him. Mrs Pardoe went straight to bed when she came home, and didn't realise that Winter had been out all night until the morning. She was convinced that something must have happened to her, since she was sure Winter wasn't That Sort, and was dithering about wondering what to do when a constable appeared with the news. That's all from the hotel, sir. Superintendent Marsh had all her things taken down to the police station."

"I've seen them," Longton told him. "Nothing there. She wasn't intending to stay long. She only brought an overnight bag. So she left her hotel at six o'clock, and presumably went to the cinema. There was the torn half of a ticket in her pocket. Any luck there?"

Barry shook his head.

"If she had been nineteen and a sex-pot, that commissionaire might have noticed her. He was eyeing all the chicks while I was questioning him. Dirty old man."

"What about her trip out to Parrington?"

"Nothing there, either. The taxis congregate in front of the station. None of them brought her out here. Nor was she seen on one of the buses during the evening. It's not a frequent service, and they tend to know most of their passengers. Strangers are noticed. There are a couple of car-hire firms, but they swear no one asked to be taken out to Parrington that evening."

Longton grunted.

"I don't suppose she walked seven miles. Which means a private car, most likely. Superintendent Marsh is having the cars at Lennard Plastics gone over. We'll have to see what that turns up."

"What, all of them?"

"The field is not very wide," said Longton thoughtfully. "That woman wasn't killed by a sex maniac. There was no trace of any sort of assault. And the weapon was stolen from the factory. So that narrows it down to someone who knew Anne Winter, and who also had access to the repair shop. It rules out the possibility that she was followed from London and since she hadn't been around these parts for a long time, it looks as though the motive is connected with the past."

"But it was her second visit, sir," Barry reminded him.

"True. And there may have been others. That is something we mustn't forget. But we still have to account for that spanner. I can't believe that it is just a coincidence that the murder weapon came from the factory and that half of the directors were connected with the dead woman."

"But why use a weapon which would lead us straight to the factory?"

"Haste," said Longton grimly. "Anne Winter's return came as a nasty shock to someone, and he snatched up the nearest weapon. Not that we were intended to find it. Our murderer didn't haul that tarpaulin off the pile of planks, invite his victim to sit on it and then bash her. I think she was probably killed in that garden, and then the body was hidden. And the weapon with it. To be disposed of later. Those builders turned up unexpectedly yesterday morning."

"So that narrows it a bit further. Who knew that the builders' lorry had broken down and the heap of stuff was likely to stay where it was for days?"

"It's your sister and her husband who can tell us that," Longton pointed out.

There was a knock on the door, and the barman put his head round.

"Phone call for the Sergeant," he announced. "It's Mr Lennard."

Longton's eyebrows rose.

"Tell him you are on your way. I want an answer to that question."

*   *   *

Rosalind was watching at a window when Geoffrey's car turned into the drive. It was impossible for her to settle that afternoon. Above everything, she wanted to talk to her husband. Thank heaven, he's home early, she thought, as she ran out to meet him.

"Leave the car out," she called. "We'll fetch Sally later. You see the police have let the builders move all that stuff."

Geoffrey pulled a face.

"I'm darned glad to see the back of that lot. For all sorts of reasons," he added grimly.

Rosalind shuddered.

"Poor Anne! I do hope they will find out who did it."

"They will. You had the Scotland Yard men here?"

"Yes. Geoffrey, I had such a surprise," she began, as they strolled towards the house.

"Not what you thought they would be?" he broke in, amused. "I've only seen the Superintendent, so far. He came to the factory on his own this afternoon. I thought he would have his minions with him."

"He has a sergeant."

"No doubt we shall meet him in due course. Longton struck me as a thorough type. His visit today was just a preliminary skirmish. Not that I could tell him anything. True enough, I saw Anne the night before she was killed, on the Tuesday, but I wasn't with her on Wednesday, which is the important time."

Rosalind's heart lifted in relief.

"Then you *were* at the factory that night?"

There was a short silence.

"You wondered, did you, Roz?"

"Well, yes," she admitted. "After all, you did tell a fib for the previous evening."

"Did you also wonder if I had killed her?" he asked.

The colour flamed up into her face.

"Geoffrey! That's a terrible thing to say. Of course I didn't. It never occurred to me. Why should you?"

He stared broodingly at her.

"No," he echoed, "why should I?"

Rosalind stared back at him in horror.

"Geoffrey, stop it!"

He relaxed a little.

"The trouble is, Roz, I was the only one who actually saw her."

"What of it? Geoffrey, you are not seriously worrying about this, are you?"

His face was still clouded.

"I was just trying to put myself in the place of the police."

"They aren't stupid and they don't jump to conclusions," she retorted heatedly. "You were at the factory all Wednesday evening."

"Yes," he said slowly, "I was."

The knowledge did not seem to comfort him.

"It's that damned spanner," he muttered.

"An outsider couldn't have got hold of it?"

Geoffrey shook his head.

"Tom Yates has a good storeman. The tools are locked up each night. He can swear that spanner was stolen on Wednesday. It wasn't there when they knocked off. Yates was in a temper about it. And he searched the whole place."

"So what?" demanded Rosalind robustly. "If it was left lying about during the day, anyone could have taken it. There are always dozens of people going in and out of the garage."

"But there aren't dozens of people who knew Anne Winter."

Rosalind had no answer to that.

"I can't think why anyone should want to kill Anne,"

she said firmly. "It must have been a sex maniac. Pure coincidence that he did it with a spanner he took from the factory."

In spite of himself, Geoffrey laughed.

"Hopeful!" he exclaimed.

"Come in and have some tea. And don't think any more about it. Leave it to the police."

"I've enough other things to worry about," he agreed, following her into the house. "The board meeting is on Monday morning. I've told Peter he will have to be there, cold or no cold. Threadwell has already hinted that I wanted Peter out of the way for the meeting we were going to hold on Thursday. No, I want the whole board there, as much as he does. I want to face it out with them, and find out who blames me for the fact that someone could steal our drawings."

"But it's not fair. They can't blame you."

"Someone has to take the blame. The shareholders will see to that, aided by Threadwell. And it will be me, unless I can do something to prevent it. There is only one hope for me, and that is to find out who really did do the job."

"But you have been over it time and again, and found nothing. What can you do over this weekend?"

"Threadwell has got hold of something. If he has, then I can. Roz, you worked at the place. Threadwell thinks it was a woman. Which boils it down to one of the tracers, or unthinkable though it is—Elsie Summers. Who gets your vote?"

"I can't answer that," said Rosalind steadily. "I was at the factory only a few weeks, and I didn't know any of the people in the drawing office. Between now and Monday, you can't work on them enough to get one of them to break down and admit it."

Geoffrey swung round.

"But it's my only hope. Don't damn my chances from the start."

"I said *you* couldn't. You are a private citizen. You can't go barging into people's homes, asking them questions. But the police can."

"It's too late for that," he replied impatiently. "If I was going to call them in, I should have done it months ago. You know why we didn't. The damage was done, and we didn't want any publicity. Maybe we were wrong, but that was the decision and it is too late to go back on it now."

"I know. I didn't mean the Broadgate police. But the Scotland Yard—"

He cut in with a bitter laugh.

"They would be pleased to be handed this one. All I should get is a flea in my ear."

Rosalind shook her head.

"We can ask them unofficially. They will have to question all sorts of people over the murder case, they might easily pick up a hint about this theft of the drawings, too."

Geoffrey stared at her.

"But why should they help us? After all, I must be one of their suspects. I can't imagine Superintendent Longton letting himself be distracted for one moment from the murder hunt."

Rosalind laughed.

"I wouldn't dare ask him," she admitted, "but his sergeant will help us, if he can. You haven't met him yet. His name is Barry Thornley, and he is my brother, Geoffrey," she ended, in a rush.

Her husband was dumbfounded.

"I've told people that I was an orphan for so long now that I have almost come to believe it myself," she went on. "I cut myself off from my family years ago. They opposed my marriage to Dick. Of course their worst fears about him were justified. That's why I couldn't go back, after he died. I was too proud. And as the years passed, it seemed more and more difficult.

It was easier to go on pretending I was alone. I'm sorry, Geoffrey. I wanted to tell you, but there didn't seem to be much point, after all this time."

"What family have you got?"

"My parents, my brother, some cousins we never saw very often. They live in Slough. My father is a research chemist. And Barry is a policeman. When I left, he was pounding a beat. Now he is a detective sergeant."

"Does Sally know?"

Rosalind shook her head.

"I never realised how much she wanted a family until I married you, Geoffrey," she admitted. "The way she took to your mother shook me. She doesn't remember her father, you know. I thought I could give her a full enough life, on my own. I was wrong. I should have made contact with my own people years ago. At least, I should have tried to find out if they wanted me back."

Geoffrey was watching her closely.

"They will."

Rosalind managed a smile.

"Barry hinted as much. It's a relief. But what about you, Geoffrey? Do you mind?"

"Mind? Roz, you idiot, I'm delighted. I don't believe in people cutting themselves off from their families. Relations can be very tiresome at times, but there is something about a family which can be a great help when you're up against it. You should have gone back to them years ago, pride or no pride. When are you going to see them?"

"I don't know. I hadn't thought about it. There has been so much happening today."

Suddenly the thought of Anne Winter lay between them.

Rosalind felt the tears spring up in her eyes and begin to run down her cheeks.

"I'll have to be quick," she sobbed. "Anne wanted to see her parents again, and she never made it. If anything happened to me, Sally would never get to know her grandparents."

Geoffrey was shaking her.

"Roz, darling, stop it. The situation is quite different. I'm here, and your brother. Sally would never be on her own. Don't let your nerves start playing you up now. Roz, what is it? Roz!"

The tears had stopped and now she was staring at him, white-faced.

"Geoffrey! It has just occurred to me. Suppose Anne's situation was even more like mine than we thought? Suppose she kept the child?"

"She never mentioned it when I talked to her."

"What has that to do with it? She wanted to re-establish contact with her parents. Wouldn't she have come alone, first, to see what sort of reception she would get? And wouldn't she have kept quiet about the child, too, and bring them round to accepting it gradually, once they had taken her back?"

"Yes," said Geoffrey heavily, "Anne would have reasoned that way. In which case—"

"In which case, that child—how old would it be? Sixteen?—that child is somewhere. On its own."

Geoffrey strode into the hall, picked up the phone and began dialling.

"It's time we had a talk with your brother," he said.

CHAPTER 10

GEOFFREY drove into Broadgate alone, to fetch Sally from his mother's house. Once he had mentioned that he must look in on Edward, Rosalind had been glad enough to stay in Parrington. Glenda's curiosity would have been more than she could endure that evening.

He felt too restless to sit idly at home. Now that the idea of uncovering the source of the information leak had taken root in his mind, he was anxious to be working at it. It was all very well enlisting the help of the police, and the chances were that Barry would come up with the truth before long, but Geoffrey was sure that there must be something which he himself had overlooked. They had made a thorough investigation when the thing happened, but it had not been thorough enough. They had missed something. It might be there, under their noses, some shred of evidence seen, noted and misinterpreted.

Perhaps if they put their heads together. . . .

He would start with Edward.

The Hardwicks lived in a house of stark ultra-modern design. Geoffrey habitually referred to it as their "glass box", a term which annoyed his half-sister considerably, but he could not deny that the view was magnificent. It looked out from the chalk cliffs, over the Channel, to the dim blue line of the coast of France. Today the sun was glinting on the small waves and the gulls were riding sedately on the water, instead of wheeling and crying through the wind.

Edward and Glenda were on the terrace at the back of the house, overlooking the sea.

"Geoffrey!" Glenda welcomed him. "How lovely to see you! But where is Rosalind?"

"She's at home. She didn't feel up to coming out," he replied, inventing a more polite excuse than the bald "She didn't want to come" which was on the tip of his tongue.

A small satisfied smile appeared at the corner of Glenda's mouth.

"Poor Geoffrey!" she purred. "So difficult for you."

Geoffrey stared at her. Glenda was getting at something, without a doubt, and she had recognised the excuse for what it was. He wondered suddenly if perhaps Rosalind's reservations about Glenda were more firmly based than on instinctive distrust of unknown in-laws.

For a moment he looked at his half-sister with new eyes and wondered if he liked her himself. Then he put the thought from him. He had far too much on his mind to bother about Glenda and whatever little scheme she was planning.

"Anyone would be upset, finding a dead body in the garden," he said sharply.

"Especially since it was Anne," said Glenda, apparently pleased that he had raised the subject. "Tell me, is Parrington crawling with Scotland Yard detectives?"

"Hardly crawling. There is a superintendent and a sergeant. I'm sure they are most competent people," he replied briefly. "Edward, I wanted a word with you."

"Oh, business," pouted Glenda. "All right, I know when I'm not wanted. Edward, give Geoffrey a drink."

She flounced off into the house. Neither of the two men stopped her.

Geoffrey lowered himself into a deck chair.

"It's about Monday, I suppose?" asked Edward, watching him carefully from behind his thick lenses.

"In a way. Look, Edward, there is going to be trouble at that meeting. We all know what Threadwell is after. We have a lot of business to discuss and it will be dealt with quickly and amicably. Then he'll raise the matter of the leak. He's going to demand a meeting of the shareholders."

Edward stood up.

"Hang on a tick. I'll get those drinks."

He lingered longer than necessary in the dining room over the selection of bottles and glasses. For the first time in years he needed a few moments to regain control of his face. It was all so nearly in his grasp, the prize for which he had striven over the years—the control of Lennard Plastics. He had slaved long hours to make himself indispensable; married advantageously and without love; schemed and planned. But not a hint of the anticipated triumph must show. Geoffrey forewarned would be forearmed. He trusted him, where he could not trust Richard Seldon, or the Colonel, or even Peter Maynard, his own cousin. The shock would be all the greater on Monday, and would destroy him.

When he reappeared on the terrace, Geoffrey had left his chair and was leaning over the parapet, gazing out to sea.

"Here we are," said Edward cheerfully. "What's your poison, Geoffrey?"

"Oh, anything," replied Geoffrey vaguely.

"Whisky?"

"Yes. Fine. Edward, there's only one thing which will spike Threadwell's guns. Coming up with the name of the culprit."

Edward looked up, surprised. This was an unexpected line of attack. It needed thought.

"How are you going to find out?" he temporised.

"I don't know," Geoffrey admitted, "but Threadwell has got hold of some evidence. If he can find something, I should be able to."

Edward shaded his eyes with his hand. Threadwell had not mentioned it to him. This also needed thinking out.

"I can't think that he knows anything definite. He may just have his suspicions. We may have slipped up over the security arrangements for the drawings, but no one could accuse us of letting things slide afterwards. We did everything we could to find out who was responsible."

Geoffrey smiled. Good old Edward! Too loyal to admit even between themselves that the responsibility for that security rested ultimately on the shoulders of the managing director.

"Leave it," Edward advised him. "There is nothing you can do between now and Monday, except wear yourself out."

He had his own ideas about the identity of the traitor, and a little bit of proof, which would be enough to frighten the guilty party into a confession. But it was no part of Edward's policy to confide his suspicions to anyone, least of all to Geoffrey. It was all filed in his orderly mind, for possible use later.

"I'd help you if I could, Geoffrey, but honestly, I haven't a clue who was responsible. There are people now who make their living out of industrial spying. And they have all sorts of odd methods. Just like proper spies. We haven't a hope of detecting them. And they will be miles away by now."

It raised an echo in Geoffrey's mind. Someone else had suggested that to him, recently. They could be right. Or was the suggestion planted to deter him from making further inquiries? Perhaps to cover guilt?

Memory hit him with a sickening lurch: he knew who had made the suggestion. Elsie Summers.

He drained his glass.

"Thanks for the drink, Edward. No doubt you are right. Say goodbye to Glenda for me. Be seeing you."

He couldn't get out quick enough. He needed to be alone, to think over the idea that a woman who had served the company for so many years, who had watched it grow from tiny beginnings, who shared—he had thought—his own absorption in it, that such a woman could sell its secrets to a competitor.

Geoffrey drove slowly into the centre of Broadgate, his mind half on the problem, and half on the crowded roads. He turned away from the sea front and came to a stop in front of a large old house, now converted into flats. He looked up at it in surprise. In his preoccupation, he had driven straight to David Kindersley's doorstep.

David took one look at his friend's face, and asked no questions. He led him into the comfortable, shabby sitting room and sat quietly while Geoffrey paced about.

"David," he burst out at last, "do you think—"

He stopped. Not even to David could he voice his suspicions of Elsie. It was no good, he would have to face her himself. But, supposing he were wrong, what would that do to her? How would she feel, after all these years of devoted service, when she knew that he could suspect her of such a crime? And what had he to go on, after all? A chance remark of her own, which she might have made, as Edward had, because it was impossible to think that one of them could be a traitor. And a hint from Stanley Threadwell, of all people. No, at this stage, he could neither speak of it to others, nor tackle Elsie.

"Lord," he muttered, "this is a foul business."

"Don't let it get you down, Geoffrey. The police will find who did it. And there is nothing that any of us can do for Anne now."

Geoffrey swung round. He had forgotten Anne, for the moment. Forgotten, too, another vicious thought which gnawed at his mind.

"The child," he said almost savagely, "she kept it."

He knew he was watching David, watching for a flicker of confirmation, the batting of an eyelid which could crumble twenty years' friendship to dust. But he could not be sure. He saw surprise, even shock, on David's face.

"Are you sure?"

"The police told me. It's a daughter. And she is living in London. David, who was the father?"

This was the moment. After the first brief shock of Anne's departure, the matter had never been discussed between them. David's hand clenched themselves into fists, the knuckles showing white under the skin.

"I don't know. I wish to heaven I did. I've wanted to know the answer to that for seventeen years."

"You've no idea? It must have happened sometime in the December, as far as I can work it out. You were with us for that last Christmas. Remember it? It was one endless round of parties."

"I remember," said David grimly.

"You loved her, too," said Geoffrey, at last voicing what had lain, unacknowledged, between them for so long. "You must have watched her. Didn't you notice anything? Between her and one of the others," he added, unable to bring himself to make the accusation. "At one of the parties . . ." he trailed off.

David was shaking his head.

"I saw nothing," he said painfully. Even now, he could not admit to Geoffrey the agony of those last months, while the preparations for the wedding were going forward. Unable to bring himself to stay away, unwilling to lose his greatest friend, yet tortured by the sight of Anne Winter, and the instinctive knowledge that for her it was a marriage without love, he had endured rather than lived through that time. Even the end, when it came, though it had shocked him, had been a relief.

It's no use, thought Geoffrey. David was never one to wear his heart on his sleeve. If he is a seducer and murderer, it will take a better man than I to surprise it out of him. And what is happening to me, that I can suspect my best friend? If David had been the father of Anne's child, there would have been no reason for him to cast her off. Or later, to kill her.

Geoffrey glanced at his watch.

"Eight o'clock. I must dash. I'm supposed to be collecting Sally."

He needed the fresh air. His treacherous brain had just reminded him that if David had taken Anne away from him, he would have lost his chance to be partner in his own business. It was all under discussion at the time, although another couple of years was to elapse before they set up their little workshop. David could offer qualifications, enthusiasm and the dream of being his own master, but nothing else. It was Geoffrey who had the money.

And even now, what would David's position be, if he had to acknowledge the paternity of Anne's child? Geoffrey might forgive him, but what about Colonel Winter? And the scandal would re-echo round the small town.

Sick at heart, Geoffrey turned the car in the direction of his mother's house.

* * *

Barry eyed Geoffrey thoughtfully. He was thinking: so this is Rosalind's second choice; and a great improvement on the other; unless he killed Anne Winter. His mother would want a detailed description of Geoffrey and he was trying to form noncommittal phrases, ready for the phone call that evening. He found himself wishing wholeheartedly that he could be sure that Geoffrey was innocent. He liked the look of him.

Prompted by Rosalind, Geoffrey was explaining about the leak of information at the factory and the dire consequences which threatened him.

"It's a cheek, expecting you to be able to help us," he concluded, diffidently.

"Blame me," said Rosalind. "It was my idea, but you are our last hope, Barry. Mr Threadwell is a terrible, ruthless man. He is determined to gain control of the company, and this business is meat and drink to him."

Virtually a hopeless proposition, thought Barry, after all this time.

"You should have called in the local police," he commented.

Geoffrey shrugged impatiently.

"Agreed. But it is too late now. We had a board meeting about it and we decided that the publicity would do us no good. After all, we couldn't prove a thing. So we would make our own inquiries, find who did it and quietly sack them. Threadwell agreed with that decision," he added bitterly.

"He would," exclaimed Rosalind. "It was just what he wanted. An excuse to accuse you of gross inefficiency."

"Anyway, we haven't found out the culprit," Geoffrey continued, "and now Threadwell is preparing to make a big issue of it. If he can force the vote on Monday, you can be sure that he will swing the shareholders' meeting his way, too. And that means I shall be edged out of control of my own factory. I shall still have my holding of shares, but someone else will be running it. Richard Seldon, no doubt. Though, I imagine, Threadwell will make sure that he has some efficient underling to prevent him wrecking the whole shoot."

"This Mr Seldon," inquired Barry, "could he have engineered the leak?"

Geoffrey shook his head.

"Most unlikely. I can't see him being subtle enough to visualise it as a long-term weapon for unseating me."

"You've known him for a long time?"

"All my life. He was a business associate of my father, years back, and he is my godfather, as a matter of fact. He was running his own business until six years ago, when we bought him out. Part of the deal was that he should have a seat on the board. And I offered him a job, too. Which was a pretty daft thing to do, as it turned out. The man's a nuisance. I don't say he couldn't do the job, if he put his mind to it, but he has an inflated idea of his own importance."

"All right, let's leave him. Who else could have got at those drawings. Where were they kept?"

"In the safe in Miss Summers' office. The trouble is that it is not much more than a steel cupboard. It is kept locked, but there are no particular security measures about the keys. She has one, and so do I. Also David Kindersley has one. And Colonel Winter. We only keep certain documents in it. Any one of us who has something in there has a key. Threadwell seems to think it was a woman who took those drawings and copied them. I can't believe that Miss Summers would do that. She has been with us from the beginning. So that brings it back to the drawing office. There are women tracers there, and someone must have handled the drawings. So it has to be one of them."

"I don't think there is much chance of my finding out before Monday," said Barry, "but I will do what I can. Presumably, whoever leaked the information was paid well for it, so we have to look for someone unexpectedly flush. I'll have a quiet word with the C.I.D. sergeant at Broadgate. He may drop on something. And you are quite right," he added, "we have to keep our eyes on everyone at Lennard Plastics, since the weapon which killed Anne Winter came from here. And we may very well uncover your traitor while we are looking for our murderer. They could even be the same person."

Geoffrey frowned.

"But Anne had nothing to do with the factory. It wasn't in existence when she left home."

"When you come to think of it," replied Barry quietly, "there's not much that we do know—yet. We have very little information about Anne Winter herself, for instance. We know she ran away from home and we know why, but we don't know who was the father of the child. Do you?"

Geoffrey shook his head.

"She wouldn't tell anyone. She wrote to me, and said it was someone we didn't know. I left it at that. At the time I was too angry to think straight, and I assumed she had gone off with him. After I had talked to her the other night and it was clear that she hadn't, I wondered if perhaps she had said that to protect him, whoever he was."

"There is no one you suspect?"

"I wouldn't know where to begin," Geoffrey replied, a shade too quickly. "Anyway, what can it matter? It's all so long ago now."

Barry gave him a straight look.

"You know as well as I do that, on the face of what evidence there is at the moment, Anne Winter was killed because someone couldn't afford to have her back in this district. She lived here all her youth, and she only did one memorable thing, and that was to get herself pregnant, and by someone who was not in a position to marry her. Of course, we may come up with some other motive, like a long-lost and lately dead relative with an immense fortune, but until we do, this is the only motive which stands out. She reappears in this district and at once she is killed. It looks to me uncommonly like blackmail."

"Blackmail?" cried Geoffrey, incredulously, "Anne a blackmailer?"

"She was obviously in a position to make life more than difficult for someone. Hence the murder."

"But she came to make it up with her parents. She was dying of leukaemia."

Barry nodded.

"The post mortem confirmed that. She hadn't long, poor soul. And she knew it. A desperate woman might not look on that sort of request as blackmail."

"Oh, God!" Rosalind broke in, her understanding leaping ahead of him, "the child!"

"Yes," said Barry, "the child. She kept it. It's a daughter. Anne Winter knew she was dying and she wanted someone to see for the girl. She didn't mention her to you?"

Geoffrey shook his head dumbly.

"She thought of her parents," Barry went on, "but her father wouldn't see her."

Geoffrey sighed.

"I told you, I phoned her that afternoon. The Colonel wouldn't listen to me. I told Anne not to give up hope. I said to leave it with me for a day or two. I was sure he would come round. If only she had told me about the child. He would have had to listen then. I would have made him."

"So," said Barry, "when her parents wouldn't see her, she must have made contact with the child's father. It was up to him to do something for the girl. And that did it. She had two phone calls on the day she died. The first was yours. Did you phone her again?"

Geoffrey shook his head.

"Then it was the murderer, more than likely," said Barry.

"But the child," Rosalind broke in, "where is she? She can't be left on her own."

"We don't know. I expect you have wondered why the newspapers haven't printed Miss Winter's name or her photograph. These won't be released until that child has been found and told. We wouldn't want her to read about her mother in the newspapers."

"But where is she?" cried Rosalind, feeling panic rising in her. Sally, she was thinking. Imagine Sally in a similar position.

"It's fairly certain she is staying with friends. She and her mother lived in a flat in Ealing. We found the address in Miss Winter's handbag. But the place is all locked up. The neighbours told us the daughter was staying with the family of a girl who goes to the same school. The trouble was, they couldn't say which school it was, so it will take a little time to trace the girl. We should have her by tomorrow."

There was the sound of a car turning into the drive. Rosalind ran to the window.

"It's your Superintendent, Barry."

He joined her at the window.

"So it is. Something must have come up to bring him along here to fetch me. Quick, before he comes in. There was a question I was to ask you both. Who knew the builders' lorry had broken down and that they weren't likely to move that heap of stuff for a few days?"

Rosalind and Geoffrey exchanged glances.

"Well, we did. And Mrs Purvis, our cleaner," she said uneasily, "and between us we must have mentioned it to a lot of people. The contractors are waiting to start on the drive, and they couldn't until that had been taken away."

"She was hidden, then?" asked Geoffrey heavily, as Rosalind went to admit the Superintendent.

Barry nodded.

"I don't think it was intended that she should be found. Or the weapon. She was just supposed to disappear. What would you have thought if you found she had left 'The Ship'?"

"That she had gone back to London."

"Exactly. And you would have left it at that."

"But what about the hotel? And her things?"

"They wouldn't have given it a second thought if someone had come in to pay the bill and collect her suitcase. But those builders came too soon, and blew the whole scheme wide open."

Longton came into the room, Rosalind behind him.

"I want Sergeant Thornley," he announced, "but while I'm here, Mr Lennard, I would like to go over a little part of your statement. The evening of the murder, you were working late in your office?"

"Yes."

"You didn't go to 'The Ship' and ask to see Anne Winter?"

"No."

Rosalind felt a spasm of fear. Surely, they would recognise innocence when they saw it? But Geoffrey seemed suddenly so tense, so wary.

"Or call back again, later, when you didn't find her the first time?"

"No."

Longton grunted, glanced round the room, then swung round on Rosalind.

"Were you living here the first week in January?"

"No," she replied, surprised, "we were on our honeymoon then."

"Ah," he said, apparently satisfied, "that would explain it."

"Explain what?" demanded Geoffrey and his voice was harsh.

"Why Anne Winter didn't see you," replied the

D

Superintendent blandly. "She stayed in Broadgate for a couple of days in January. But no one seems to have seen her. None of your circle that is. I suppose she discovered that you were away and didn't bother looking up anyone else. Come along, Sergeant. Good evening, both."

Barry followed his superior out to the car. He recognised the game the old devil was playing. And he had seen more than one clever murderer break under the strain. Now the old man was going after Geoffrey Lennard. . . .

With a shock he realised that he no longer had an open mind. It mattered very much for Geoffrey to be proved innocent.

CHAPTER 11

BARRY turned the police car into the dingy London suburban road. The houses were Victorian, large, converted into flats and all rather the worse for wear.

"That'll be it," said Superintendent Longton, "where the divisional car is parked."

The doors of the other car opened as Barry drew into the kerb behind it. People got out, a plain-clothes man, a woman and a girl. Barry and Longton went over to them.

"Sergeant Davies, sir," the plain-clothes man introduced himself, "this is Mrs Matthews. The girl has been staying with them."

Longton nodded.

"Sorry about this, Mrs Matthews." He eyed the girl. "She knows?"

Mrs Matthews, a thin woman, with a lined, kindly face, glanced at the girl.

"Yes," she said in a low voice, "I have told her. Fenella, this is Superintendent Longton."

Fenella Winter stepped forward. She was tall, certainly a head taller than her mother. She had Anne's fair hair and brown eyes, but there the likeness ended. Fenella was altogether more robust than her mother, and already, at the age of sixteen, there was an air of composure, even of command, about her.

There was a hint of tears in the large eyes, but she had herself well in hand.

"How do you do?" she said in a clear voice.

Longton, who had a daughter of roughly the same age himself, said gruffly, "I'm sorry about this, Miss Winter, but we want to have a glance through your mother's things."

Fenella nodded.

"I understand. Please go ahead."

They all went into the house, up the stairs to the first floor flat which was Fenella's home. Inside, there was the suffocating air of closed rooms in hot weather. Fenella threw up the sash window in the living room.

"It will soon clear," she said.

The place was neat and clean. The furniture was slightly shabby, but cared for, and brightened with new cushion covers and curtains. There was one bedroom, with twin beds, a bathroom and a newly painted kitchen.

"Have you lived here long?" asked Longton.

"Four years," Fenella told him. "The flat we had before was not very nice. And we had to share a bathroom. But Mother got a promotion, so we could afford something better."

"Tell me about your mother," he invited, "we don't know much about her. What did she do for a living?"

"She worked at Willings, the department store in Oxford Street. She was an assistant buyer, in China and Glass."

"How long had she worked there?"

"I'm afraid I don't know. As long as I can remember."

Longton glanced at Barry, now seated at the table, his notebook open before him.

"We can check on that. Did your mother ever speak of her family?"

"Never, until recently. I didn't even know that she came from near Broadgate until she went last January."

"Do you know why she went?"

Fenella nodded.

"She was in hospital last December. They did some tests. The results came through at the beginning of January," the girl's eyes glistened, but she fought back the tears. "My mother was going to die, Superintendent. She said she wanted to go away for a few days, to think things over. It was then that she told me that she came from a village near Broadgate. She went down there for a couple of days. By herself."

"Did she intend to make contact with her family?"

"No. That came later. She was getting worse, and she was afraid that she wouldn't live long enough to see me through my schooldays. She was worrying about who would look after me." Fenella hesitated, then went on in her clear voice, "I didn't want her to make it up with her family if it was going to embarrass her."

"So you knew about—your circumstances?"

"Yes. She told me, but I think I had guessed long ago. She called herself Mrs Winter, but she never mentioned my father. There was another girl at school whose father was dead, and she knew quite a lot about him, and there were photographs and things, which we hadn't got. I wondered perhaps if he had just left her when I was a baby, but that didn't seem to fit, either. It wasn't a great surprise when she told me the truth."

"Did she tell you who was your father?"

Longton's quiet voice betrayed nothing of the excitement which lay behind the question. Barry looked up expectantly from his notebook. One word from this girl and the case might be cracked. Mrs Matthews, who knew nothing of the circumstances, caught the feeling of tension and gazed at the girl, rapt.

But Fenella shook her head.

"I asked her, but she said it was better for me not to know. She had never told anyone. I begged her to tell me, but she refused. She said no good would come of it."

"That was a pity," commented Longton. "However, let's leave that for a moment. Let's get back to your mother's first visit to Broadgate. Did she mention that she had met anyone she knew, while she was there?"

"No. She didn't say much about her trip. But she seemed better in herself, more settled."

"Did she receive any letters from Broadgate, after the visit?"

"No. But then she never had any personal letters, except postcards from her staff when they were on holiday, and things like that."

Longton nodded.

"I see. When did she decide to make the second visit?"

Fenella's eyes dropped.

"A month ago, she made another visit to the specialist. After it, she said she had to make some arrangements for me. We argued about it. I didn't know how the family would receive her and I didn't want her to risk getting hurt, just for me. We argued for weeks. Then, last Friday, she came home from work with her mind made up. She had some holiday due and she would spend it in Broadgate. She said she wanted to see them, herself, before the end."

"She didn't write to them first?"

"No. I suggested that. I thought that if they were going to snub us, it wouldn't be so bad if they did it in writing, rather than face to face. But Mother said she would approach them through someone else, a friend."

"Ah!" Longton pounced on it. "This friend? Who was it?"

"Some man, I think. I don't know his name."

"Did your mother tell you anything about him?"

Fenella hesitated.

"No, but there was something in the way she referred to him. I did wonder," she said uncertainly.

"You thought he might be your father?"

"I don't know. I thought he might be. But in that case, I couldn't understand why Mother said it was better for me not to know who he was. I suppose he must be married."

"He is," said Longton. "So she went to Broadgate."

"On Tuesday morning."

"Did you hear from her?"

The tears rushed into Fenella's eyes. She bit her lip and shook her head, not trusting herself to speak.

"We shall find out who did it, young lady," Longton assured her with grim confidence. "But it will make it a lot easier for us if you can remember anything special that your mother said about going to Broadgate, or the people she hoped to see when she was there. Cast your mind back. The smallest detail, which might seem unimportant to you, might mean a lot to us."

His words had steadied the girl.

"There was one thing, Superintendent. A remark she made, oh, last Sunday, I think. I can't even remember the context now. But it was something about devotion and never marrying after losing your first love. It's all very vague, but from the way she said it, I guessed it meant something special to her. I don't know why, but I connected it with Broadgate, and someone in her past. I don't know if that is of any help?" she ended uncertainly.

"Could be. Perhaps we shall find something among your mother's papers which will help us."

Longton made to rise, but the girl's eyes were fixed on him intently, and he dropped back into his chair.

"Superintendent," Fenella began, "Mother's family— that is, my family—how did they receive her?"

Longton sighed. It was a pity, but the girl had to be told.

"They didn't get a chance to see her."

"But she went on Tuesday, and it happened on Wednesday evening, didn't it?"

"The friend, whom she approached, had not managed to arrange a meeting."

"You mean, they didn't want us," said Fenella.

"They didn't know about you. I'm sure they will be very anxious to have you with them when they do." Longton had a sudden vision of Daphne Winter and mentally crossed his fingers. "Your mother's death has shaken them very much," he added, with perfect truth.

Fenella's mouth set in a determined line.

"If they didn't want her, they won't want me either. I can do without them."

Mrs Matthews ran to the girl and put her arm round her shoulders.

"Don't think about it, now, Fenella. Leave it to sort itself out. And you are welcome to stay with us for as long as you like."

Longton stood up.

"We'll get on with our search, if you don't mind. Don't worry about your family, Miss, you'll be all right."

Barry closed his notebook.

"There are others, too, sir. Mrs Lennard was very concerned about Miss Winter when I told her about her."

Longton frowned.

"I'm sure she was," he said shortly.

Fenella roused herself.

"Mother kept all her papers in a box in the bottom of her wardrobe. There are some old letters in there, too."

Barry followed his superior into the bedroom.

The box was there, all right, but it was empty.

Fenella came running at their call.

"But I don't understand," she said, "there were quite a few papers in there. I saw them many a time, but I never touched them myself. Mother must have taken them with her, but I can't think why."

"There is nothing among her things at the hotel," Longton told her. "It looks as though someone has been in here, and taken them. Who else has a key?"

"No one. Only Mother and me. I have mine, and she took hers with her."

Longton looked at Barry.

"No key either on her or in her possession at 'The Ship', sir."

"That's it, then," said the Superintendent, "the murderer took her key and came here to search the place at his leisure." He turned to the plain-clothes man from the local Division, "Sergeant Davies, I'd be obliged if you'd get on the blower and ask for a couple of chaps. This is going to take a bit of time. We'll have to question all the neighbours." Sergeant Davies went out smartly. "Thornley, see what dabs you can lift off that wardrobe. Miss Winter, come round with me and let's see if we can decide what has been disturbed and what hasn't."

It was soon clear that the searcher had confined himself to the bedroom.

"He found what he was after pretty quickly," commented Longton. "No doubt, that box of papers in the wardrobe. However, we'll have a good look round while we are on," he added, entering the kitchen, Fenella at his heels. "What's that?" he demanded.

He was pointing at a lady's handbag, dangling by its handle from the back of a chair.

"That? It's Mother's every-day bag. The one she used for going to the store."

"Let's have a look at it. No, don't you touch it. There may be prints we want on it. Let me see."

Carefully he opened the handbag. Inside was an empty purse, a few items of make-up, a comb—and a photograph. Fenella peered over Longton's shoulder.

"Who is that? I've never seen it before. Do you know who it is?"

"Yes," said Longton with grim satisfaction, "I do."

It was a recent snapshot of Geoffrey Lennard.

* * *

Rosalind and Geoffrey had hardly finished breakfast the next morning when Superintendent Longton arrived. He was grim-faced and his eyes passed over her coldly as she let them in.

"Your husband in?" he demanded.

Rosalind moistened suddenly dry lips.

"Yes. I'll call him."

"We want to talk to him alone."

She cast a quick glance at her brother, but Barry's face was expressionless.

"Please go into the study. I'll tell my husband that you are here."

Geoffrey was already at the dining room door, his last cup of coffee in his hand, the morning paper tucked under his arm. The usual Saturday routine, coffee and the news in the peace of his own den, thought Rosalind automatically. She glanced at the hard face of the older man, and her heart began to beat painfully. Geoffrey held out his cup and the paper. She took them without speaking.

Sally came running in from the kitchen, but stopped short when she saw the strangers.

Rosalind pushed her before her through the door, back into the kitchen.

"Go out in the garden for a bit," she told her, "and don't forget to feed the rabbit. He'll be wanting his breakfast, too."

The child ran out into the sunshine. Rosalind dropped into a chair, scarcely able to breathe for the pounding of her heart. The house was silent. No matter how she strained her ears, she could hear nothing, although she knew that in the study Longton must be talking in his dry, deadly voice.

She could not have said why she was so afraid. The Superintendent's parting shot yesterday had jarred on her, but it was not enough to bring her into this state of fear. Geoffrey could not have had any part in the killing of Anne Winter. That, she believed wholeheartedly. She knew the police must question everyone who had any connection with the dead woman; question and question again, until the vital shred of evidence came to light. And she would not have it any other way. Normally, she was not a vengeful person, but it mattered very much that the murderer of the unfortunate Anne should be brought to justice.

Yet, from the moment that she had opened the door to the police this morning, she had been possessed with an unreasoning, instinctive fear. She sat at the table in the bright, newly painted kitchen and trembled.

In the study there was a silence. Then Geoffrey handed back to Longton the photograph which had been found in Anne Winter's old handbag.

"It was taken last summer, Superintendent. That is my mother's garden."

"Who took it?"

"My mother. Superintendent, why are you interested in this snap? Where did you get it?"

Longton permitted himself a grim smile.

"There is only one answer to both those questions, Mr Lennard. It was in the possession of Anne Winter."

Geoffrey stared at him.

"But how had she got hold of it?"

"We thought you might have given it to her."

"I did not. Our discussion when I saw her on Tuesday was too serious to take in giving snapshots."

"Oh, I didn't mean on Tuesday," Longton told him, blandly, "she had it before then."

"But that's impossible. She couldn't have had it."

"I assure you she did. You can't explain how?"

"No," said Geoffrey shortly, "I can't."

"You say your mother took the snap. Who else would be likely to have a copy?"

"How should I know?" retorted Geoffrey irritably, "I don't know who Mother gives snaps to."

"Then we shall have to ask her. But you had a print?"

"Yes."

"Only one?"

"Yes."

"Do you think you could find it?"

Geoffrey searched the drawers of his desk, but there was no sign of the photograph.

"I'm afraid I can't lay my hand on it," he admitted, reluctantly. "My wife might be able to."

"So she might," agreed Longton. "Not that it really matters, Mr Lennard. Even if you could find it, it wouldn't prove you never had another print, would it?"

Geoffrey set his teeth.

"No," he said, "it wouldn't. Is there anything else, Superintendent?"

"Oh, yes, quite a lot of things. I should like to go back over the part of your statement which deals with Wednesday night—the night of the murder. You stayed late at the factory, working?"

"Yes. We were supposed to be having a board meeting the next day. I was doing some last-minute jobs."

"You didn't drive into Broadgate to see Anne Winter?"

"No," said Geoffrey steadily, hoping he had not hesitated, and feeling a trickle of sweat rolling down his neck. He dared not raise his hand to wipe it off.

"You didn't pick her up and take her out in your car?"

"No."

It was a relief to be back on firm ground, where the truth could be told.

"We found a few hairs from her head and a trace of her face powder in your car."

"She was in the car on Tuesday evening," said

Geoffrey easily, "I took her out to dinner. I told you that right at the start."

Longton wagged his head.

"So, you did, Mr Lennard. But it's Wednesday night I'm interested in."

"She wasn't with me."

"So you say."

"It's the truth," cried Geoffrey, nettled.

"Did you also drive to London that night, to her flat, to search it?"

Geoffrey stared at him.

"To—*what*? Superintendent, what is this?"

"The flat was searched and some private papers taken," Longton told him, "the chances are that it was done on the night of the murder."

"I didn't even know where she lived."

"No? There was the address in her handbag—and her front door key. Which is missing."

A moment ago, Geoffrey had been filled with anger, but now it ebbed and he felt calm. He understood only too well the direction of the Superintendent's suspicions. Understood, but could not believe. He felt detached from the scene, as though he were an outsider, looking in on it. But he was conscious of a sense of danger, and of the cold eyes of his inquisitor.

"Superintendent," he said, "I am afraid that I must decline to answer any more questions on this subject until my solicitor is present."

Barry bent his head over his notebook, to hide his expression. Bravo, Geoffrey, he was thinking, that's the one weapon to use against Longton; it won't stop the old devil hunting you down, but it will put a damper on his cat-and-mouse tactics.

Longton shrugged.

"As you wish," he said indifferently. "I must tell you that I have here a warrant to search this house." He produced it from his pocket and held it out to Geoffrey.

Rosalind came flying out of the kitchen when she heard the study door open.

"They are going to search the house, Rosalind," Geoffrey said calmly.

"What are they looking for?" she demanded, unable to bite back the words.

Neither of the detectives answered.

"Among other things," Geoffrey replied, "for the key to Anne's flat."

Rosalind's hands flew to her mouth.

"Geoffrey!" she cried and, oblivious of the others, flung herself into his arms.

The search yielded nothing.

"We will have to try your office," Longton commented, "but you were probably intelligent enough to get rid of that key. Pity you overlooked that photograph. For you, that is. Do you mind telling me where you were last night?"

Geoffrey stared, at the switch of the questioning.

"At what time?" he countered warily.

"Oh, from, say, seven o'clock on."

Geoffrey glanced at Rosalind.

"I went over to Broadgate, to fetch my step-daughter. I left about half-past six. Straight after you, in fact."

"And what time did you return?"

"It would be getting on for nine, I suppose." He glanced at his wife again, and Rosalind nodded. "It was past Sally's bedtime, and my wife was a bit put out," he added.

"You didn't go with him, Mrs Lennard?"

"I wanted to look in on my brother-in-law, to talk over a bit of business," Geoffrey answered for her. "That is Mr Hardwick, whom you saw at the factory."

"You went straight there?"

"Yes. I stayed about twenty minutes."

"Where did you go then?"

"I stopped at Mr Kindersley's flat for a few minutes,

then went to my mother's house to pick up Sally. Superintendent, what is this about?"

"I'm not wasting either your time or mine," replied Longton. "I suppose you didn't think of calling on Mr Seldon, too? In case you were thinking of denying it," he added savagely, "let me tell you that your car was seen standing outside his house at a quarter-past eight last night."

Rosalind, her hand clutching Geoffrey's arm, felt him stiffen.

"As a matter of fact I did call there," he admitted. "We had had words during the afternoon, at the factory. I thought I might persuade him to see a bit of sense. I had to pass his place on my way to pick up Sally. I was already late, but I thought I might as well stop and have a word with him. But he wasn't there. I suppose he had gone to the hospital to see his wife. Can't you ask him?"

"No," said Longton heavily, "I can't. Richard Seldon was murdered last night."

Richard Seldon's house lay in a quiet road, well away from the sea front with its crowds of holidaymakers. But this morning there was a small crowd of onlookers, attracted by the coming and going of police cars. There was a large house on the corner, empty, its garden a tall wilderness, waiting for the developer's bulldozer. Seldon's place was the next one, old like its neighbour, and surrounded with a large garden. This part of the town had been built before commuting to Town by a fast train was ever thought of. One by one, the old houses were being swept away, to make room for blocks of flats.

Barry parked neatly behind one of the local police cars, then followed his superintendent up the drive and into the house. They met Superintendent Marsh on the porch.

"We've just about finished here," he greeted them. "Any luck?"

"He's badly shaken," said Longton with a grim smile,

"but he's going to be a hard nut to crack. He won't break down without more evidence."

Marsh turned back into the house and they followed him into the room overlooking the back garden where the body of the dead man had been found, early that morning, by the cleaner. All that remained were chalk marks on the floor, where the body had lain.

Marsh looked down at them.

"Seldon was attacked from behind, with a poker from that fireplace. One good hard blow finished him, but there was another to make sure. Just like Anne Winter."

"Same murderer," growled Longton. "Unless I'm totally wrong."

Superintendent Marsh did not comment. If the Murder Squad wanted to look on this one as theirs, that suited him. He and his force had enough on their hands with the swollen summer population of the town.

"There is no sign of a forced entry," he said, "so Seldon must have admitted his murderer."

Longton was prowling about the room.

"What about the time? What does the Doc say?"

"At a guess sometime before midnight, but he hopes to do better when he has done the autopsy. One of the neighbours saw him come home just before eight. He had been to the hospital, to see his wife. Woman two doors down. She was working in her garden. The same one who saw the Bentley."

"Lennard says he knocked and couldn't get a reply," commented Longton, "but then, he would. He's a cool one. As soon as we faced him with it, he came out with the explanation—pat. And he volunteered that he and Seldon had had a bust-up at the factory that afternoon. He would know someone would tell us fast enough, so he got in first." He strolled to the window. "What's in those sheds?"

Two large wooden sheds were visible at the side of the garden.

Marsh shrugged.

"Nothing much. One is full of junk, bits from Seldon's old factory, I should think. The other one is empty. According to the cleaner, Peter Maynard keeps his boat in there in the winter. Of course, it's tied up in the harbour now. Maynard lives in one of those new flats over the back." He gestured vaguely towards the fence.

Longton nodded.

"I went there. He's nursing a cold. Bit of a pity that they are pulling all these big houses down to put up those rabbit hutches."

"Oh, I don't know, it's progress. I wish they would hurry up and do something about that house next door to this. They are going to build a block of flats there, but they are waiting for planning permission. I don't like empty houses at this time of the year. We get our share of undesirables here, sleeping rough and making trouble. A house like that is just their drop."

A constable came in, to claim Superintendent Marsh's attention.

"Nothing much we can do here, Sergeant," said Longton briskly. "We had best get back to the station."

Marsh had given them a small room at the back of the building.

"Pokey," observed Longton sourly, "but I suppose it is the best he can do. While they are doing all that rebuilding, it's a pity they can't do something for the police, too."

Barry did not venture a comment. He recognised the symptoms. Superintendent Longton was niggled and was venting it on his surroundings. One misplaced word would bring it down on his own head.

"It's a mess," said Longton. "Take either murder separately and you can make sense of it, with a motive neatly tied to Geoffrey Lennard. He gets married, and almost immediately the ex-fiancée turns up, complete with full-grown child. Enough to upset any man, especially if there had been any hanky-panky in the past. Then take Seldon. The man has been causing trouble for Lennard, and is trying to grab his job. They have a bust-up and Lennard bashes him. That makes Lennard out to be some sort of loony who murders anyone who inconveniences him. Which I don't believe for a moment. If Lennard murdered them both, there has to be some connection—some common motive—between the two crimes. And I've damn-all evidence against him. Blow it, I might even believe his story if it wasn't as plain as the nose on your face that he is lying his head off."

Barry acknowledged that it was a major snag that he himself was convinced that Geoffrey was not telling the whole of the truth.

"His trouble," Longton went on, warming to the subject, "is that he isn't used to telling lies and it goes against the grain."

"I agree, sir, that he is lying," said Barry carefully, "but it doesn't follow that the whole of his story is made up. Only part of it."

Longton eyed him.

"But which part, my lad? Only the most important. The night of the murder, in fact. Well, we will see about that. That car of his is pretty conspicuous. He will sing a different tune when we face him with evidence that he was in Broadgate that night. Not to mention if we can dig up a witness in Ealing who saw the Bentley there, too. The people who live in those flats don't own recent models of expensive cars, and someone would have seen it, no matter what time of the night it was there."

"He might not have used it," Barry pointed out.

"No," agreed Longton, "and your sister's little run-about wouldn't attract attention, if he took that instead. But don't count on it."

Barry took the warning as a challenge.

"I don't think he's our man," he said boldly.

Longton's eyebrows rose.

"Don't you, indeed?" he growled. "I shouldn't have given you the option of staying on this case. I should have packed you straight back to town."

"That's up to you, sir," returned Barry, refusing to be drawn. "Maybe I am being unduly influenced by the fact that he is my sister's husband, but I think I would doubt his guilt anyway."

"You are entitled to your opinion," replied the Superintendent sarcastically, "but would you mind telling me how you arrive at that conclusion?"

Barry felt the colour rise into his face. He was well aware that he was doing himself no good at all by opposing Longton. Common sense and experience told him that Longton was a senior officer who made few mistakes. Against his trained and impartial intellect, Barry could offer little more than instinct and half-analysed emotion. But he could not—would not—back down now.

Then it occurred to him that in the normal course of events, a suspect in Geoffrey's position would be at the local station, "helping the police in their inquiries". But he was not. And it could not be because of his position as a well-known citizen. Longton was no respecter of persons. The only explanation was that Longton himself had serious doubts.

"There is no real evidence against him at all," Barry said firmly. "Everything he has told us which touches Anne Winter could be true. He could be lying about his movements on the night of her death for reasons which have nothing to do with the murder. We have found traces of her in his car. But he claims that he drove her out to dinner the night before. Now that is something we have been able to check. The Bentley was in the car park of the hotel where they ate. And the waiter who served them doesn't remember anything particular about them, so they weren't quarrelling."

"She was taken to Parrington somehow or other,"

Longton reminded him, "and there isn't a trace of her in any of the cars belonging to the other people who knew her and also work at that factory. She didn't go by taxi or by bus. It's too far to walk, and no one seems to own any other form of transport. But she could have gone in the Bentley."

"Would that convince a jury?"

Longton shrugged.

"But the main thing which makes me think we are wasting our time with Geoffrey Lennard," Barry pressed home his little advantage, "is that the motive isn't strong enough. If he were the father of her child, there would have been no reason for him to cast the mother off in the first place. She went off of her own accord. Maybe they had quarrelled and she suddenly decided she couldn't marry him, at any price. He might be mad at her, but he wouldn't have anything to fear from her."

"What about that photograph? He couldn't have given it to her in January because he wasn't here. But he must have been in touch with her."

"If he was the one to give it to her," Barry pointed out, and was gratified by the sudden narrowing of his superior's eyes.

"You've a point there," admitted Longton. "And the snap itself doesn't help either way. There are only two clear sets of prints on it. One is Anne Winter's. The other is unidentified. All the rest are blurred. So she was in touch with someone else round here?"

"Or it was planted. That flat was searched. The photograph could have been left deliberately. And if Geoffrey Lennard was the one who searched that flat, how come he overlooked it?"

"Murderers make mistakes. That's how we catch them. The searcher hadn't bothered after finding the box in the wardrobe. He thought he had the lot. Anything else, Sergeant?"

"There was another man interested in her. That

dumb blonde down at the hotel is pretty dim, but she didn't think the man who called twice that night, looking for Winter, was Lennard, when I showed her the photographs. She hovered between Maynard, Kindersley and the Colonel himself."

"It can't have been Maynard. He was laid up. The caretaker's wife was in and out of his flat, nursing him, and his car never left the garage. He almost collapsed when he got home, and the caretaker, Jones, had put it away for him, and still had the keys. Both Kindersley and the Colonel have the vague sort of alibi, unprovable in every direction. The sort which convince juries that we have picked on an innocent daftie who doesn't know enough to come in out of the rain," he added thoughtfully, "the sort a really bright murderer might think up."

"Then there's Seldon's murder," Barry went on, elated by the knowledge that he had caught the Superintendent's interest, "there ought to be a better connection between him and Lennard and Winter."

"We haven't started to dig there," Longton commented, "and remember that, however unlikely it seems, we can't overlook the possibility that, thinking he's got away with one murder, he took the same way out for a different difficulty. On the face of it, Lennard's only quarrel with Seldon is over the factory, and Winter had nothing to do with that. But she was the daughter of another of the directors. Lennard may have got her down here to influence the Colonel, and killed her when she wouldn't play. Not that there is a shred of evidence even to suggest that. No, Sergeant, your point is taken. Lennard is the obvious suspect, but there are grounds for doubt—at the moment. I admit that I haven't pulled him in because I need more to face him with. The moment I get my hands on a bit of evidence, I shall take him. But until then, and certainly for the next twenty-four hours, you may go ahead on your own. Go after the others, by all means. Then we'll see who is right."

"That's very good of you, sir," Barry murmured.

"This case is going to make or break you, Sergeant," Longton told him, wolfishly, "and take this for a parting thought : has it crossed your mind that Geoffrey Lennard might be a bigamist?"

"First of all, I want statements from Seldon's business associates," Longton went on, "apart from Lennard, that is. Narrowed your field a lot, hasn't it? The number of people who knew Anne Winter *and* could have pinched that spanner has come down a good deal. You can take the car. I've enough to keep me occupied here."

He dismissed Barry with a wave of his hand.

CHAPTER 12

LONGTON was being decent, letting him have his head, thought Barry, as he drove away from the police station, but it wasn't only a personal thing. The Old Man had a passionate concern for justice. He himself might centre his suspicions on Geoffrey Lennard, but he would never close his mind against contradictory evidence. All the same, when—if—he found some, he would have to put it over carefully if he wanted to make his career in the C.I.D.

His first call was on David Kindersley. He found him at home, apparently brooding over the death of Seldon, and glad to see anyone, even a police officer.

"This is a terrible business," he burst out, "poor old Richard. I couldn't believe it when Geoffrey phoned me. I suppose it was some burglar?"

Barry shook his head.

"No, sir. Nothing is missing, as far as the charwoman can tell. Of course, he may have had a lot of money in the house, of which she knew nothing. But there is no sign of a search."

"Good God!" said David, "then why was he killed?"

"The murderer used the same method as the one

which killed Anne Winter. The weapon was a poker, this time. When two people belonging to the same circle are killed in the same way within a few days of each other, it is not very surprising that we should link the crimes."

David stared at him.

"But what connection can Anne have had with Richard? Oh, he knew her in the past, naturally, but all that is a long time ago. Richard was as surprised as any of us when he heard she had come back. But his wife was taken ill that night and he was too concerned with her to bother about Anne."

"What was his state of mind yesterday, Friday, when he was at work?"

David groaned.

"His state of mind? Bloody, as usual. Sergeant, I might as well tell you, because the others won't be able to hide it. It's no secret that Richard Seldon and I were the proverbial chalk and cheese. We had to work together and we fought, day in, day out. But I'm damned sorry he has made an end like that."

"Would you mind giving me an account of your movements last night?"

"No, I don't mind. Not that it will help you much. Or me either," David said despondently. "I was here. I didn't go out."

"Have you anyone to support that?"

"No. This house is divided up into three flats, there is no caretaker, and I hardly ever see my neighbours. I don't go out much. I like my own company. That's the best I can do for you. Oh, Geoffrey Lennard was here for a few minutes, at about eight. But no one else."

"In other words," said Barry deliberately, "your account of last night is the same as for the night Anne Winter was killed. On both occasions you were at home, you didn't go out, you saw no one."

David looked at him for a moment, his face closed and expressionless.

"Yes," he said at last, "I'm afraid it is. But you must be wrong, Sergeant. There can be no connection between the murders. If Seldon had known anything about Anne which had made him worth murdering, he would have blabbed it all over the town."

"Which means that he was killed for other reasons. Such as—someone who wanted to scotch his opposition on the board of Lennard Plastics, once and for all?"

"If you are hinting that Geoffrey killed him," said David bleakly, "you couldn't be more wrong. Agreed Seldon was out to make trouble, but it was Threadwell who was the power behind him. Now Seldon is out of the way, Threadwell will adjust his plan accordingly. No, if Geoffrey was out to safeguard his position in the firm by resorting to murder, the logical victim would be Stanley Threadwell. There is another point, too. Seldon's holding in the company may come on to the market now. He couldn't sell them while he lived. That was part of the agreement when we took his firm over. But his widow can do what she likes with them, I imagine. And Threadwell will be after them. No, I can't see that it would be in Geoffrey's interest to put Seldon out of the way."

"And what about Anne Winter?"

"It's nonsense to suggest that Geoffrey could have done that," replied David curtly.

"Someone did. You knew her, too. What was she like?"

The muscles round David's mouth tightened.

"Yes, I knew her. I was just Geoffrey's friend. She hardly noticed me."

"You know she kept the child, and raised it, struggle though it was?"

David nodded.

"Yes, that was like Anne. I would have expected her to do that."

Barry got nothing more from David Kindersley. He went away dissatisfied. Kindersley knew far more than he would admit, of that he was convinced. But the block seemed to be loyalty to Geoffrey Lennard. And that, Barry acknowledged sadly, was no help to him, although Longton would be gratified by it. Worse, he would have to tell him.

He drove out to the clifftop house of the Hardwicks. The drive was wedged with cars, and from the open windows of the house came a babble of talk.

A cocktail party, of all things! thought Barry glumly.

He was shown into a small room, off the hall, which he took to be Edward Hardwick's study. A few moments later, Glenda came to him, her lovely face marred by an expression of acute vexation.

"Is this really necessary?" she burst out, in place of a greeting. "Couldn't it have waited till Monday? I've a house full of people."

"This is a murder case, Mrs Hardwick," Barry told her shortly.

The vexation on Glenda's brows deepened.

"Oh, yes, poor Richard," she said perfunctorily. "Very shocking. But I can't see what it has to do with us, and this party has been arranged for weeks. It would be ridiculous to put it off. He wasn't even a relative. But my brother can be very unreasonable."

Barry hid a smile. He gathered that Geoffrey had said a few sharp words over Glenda's party when his godfather was lying suddenly dead.

"Your husband was one of his associates," he said mildly, "I shan't keep him long."

"I should hope not," snapped Glenda, and flounced out.

Edward Hardwick raised none of his wife's objections to Barry's presence, though his eyebrows shot up when he was asked for an account of his movements for the previous evening.

"Of course, I realise that you have your duty to do," he said coldly, "but it seems a little unusual."

"At this stage of the investigation," hinted Barry, and left it hanging in mid-air, unsaid.

Edward unbent a little.

"I quite understand. As a matter of fact, my wife and I were at home all yesterday evening. I came home about seven o'clock. I was working late. We have an important meeting on Monday. So I am afraid we can be of no assistance to you. We know the Seldons, naturally, but they are hardly our type of people. We don't mix much socially with any of the other directors of Lennard Plastics. We don't find them congenial company. Except the Threadwells, of course. They are different. No, I'm afraid we are a dead loss to you, Sergeant. We can't help you, any more than we would over poor Anne Winter. We are a pair of home birds, my wife and I."

Barry was thinking that he had never seen anything less like a home bird than Glenda Hardwick. He was also remembering the first C.I.D. superintendent whom he had worked under, a wiley old-timer who warned his young protegé that a witness who began a statement with "As a matter of fact" very often followed it up with a whacking great lie.

"Mr Threadwell is here now, if you would like to have a word with him," Edward was saying.

"Thank you, sir, it would save me a wasted journey out to his place. He was next on my list. But one thing more, before you go. How did Seldon act at work yesterday? Was he the same as usual, would you say? Or had he, perhaps, something on his mind?"

Edward permitted himself a thin smile.

"I was too busy to pay much attention to anyone, yesterday, Sergeant. Seldon did come into my office at one point. He was complaining about irresponsibility in young people, but I don't know to whom he was referring. If, indeed, to anyone in particular. It was one of his themes, you know. I'm afraid I cut him short. He took himself off when he saw I wouldn't listen. I never saw him again."

Stanley Threadwell was fetched. Barry looked at him

with interest. So this was the man who was threatening Geoffrey. Threadwell's face was flushed, and he grasped a glass of whisky in his fat hand, but the small eyes were sharp. A typical tycoon, thought Barry, and no doubt the owner of that Rolls-Royce outside, and as dangerous a man as you would meet in a day's march.

"A shocking business, Sergeant. A burglar, I imagine. There's no telling what those fellows will get up to nowadays."

"Not a burglar, sir."

The shrewd eyes were not surprised.

"Indeed? Is there any help I can give you, Sergeant?"

"I'm asking all his associates for statements of their movements last night, sir."

"Including me? That's easy. I was in Town, at a dinner party. Here, I'll write down the name and address of my host. I'm not your murderer."

"I didn't say you were, sir," replied Barry woodenly. "This is just routine. When did you last see Mr Seldon?"

"Let's see. Thursday, when I came in for the meeting which was cancelled, he wasn't there. He'd gone to the hospital to see his wife. Before that, I was in the factory on Tuesday. Yes, I had a word with him then, poor fellow."

"What was his state of mind then?"

The small mouth pouted.

"As usual, I suppose. He wasn't a very sensible man, poor old Seldon. No tact and didn't know when to keep his mouth shut. You know the type. I've no doubt that was what finished him."

Nothing doing here, thought Barry. This one can get what he wants without stepping outside the law. And Hardwick doesn't look as though he has enough blood in him to resort to murder. Ink in his veins, more like, and about as much heart and feeling as a stone. He, too, would gain his ends by other means. Yet, he is ruthless, too, and might swat another human being down like a fly.

Passing through the hall again, he glimpsed, through the open dining room door, a laden table. It reminded him that it was past one o'clock and he was hungry. But there was so much to do, and suddenly time was pressing on him. So many people to see. And the minutes and hours relentlessly moving past. But somewhere, there must be a hint. . . .

On an impulse, he drove out to Parrington, to his sister's house. He was shocked by her appearance when she came to the door. She was pale and there were dark circles under her eyes.

"Geoffrey's out," she said, "he's taken Sally into Broadgate."

"Roz, are you all right?"

For a moment she hesitated, then her face crumpled like that of a child, and the tears came. Barry put his arm round her and led her into her kitchen, pushing her gently into a chair. He busied himself with the kettle and tea cups while she wept.

By the time the tea was made, she was drying her eyes.

"I'm sorry," she muttered.

He set a steaming cup before her.

"I'm being daft," said Rosalind, "but it was that bit on the wireless."

Barry sat very still.

"What was it?"

"A police notice, before the News, just now. Asking for witnesses of an accident in Broadgate, involving a Bentley. Barry, I know Geoffrey hasn't had an accident, but it seemed so—odd. There aren't many Bentleys round here, and it was for the night Anne was killed. It was stupid of me, but I was so afraid."

Barry sighed.

"You always did have a strong instinct, Roz. It hasn't let you down. There wasn't any accident. What they want is someone who will swear they saw Geoffrey's car in Broadgate that night. Away from the factory, that is."

"So it's a trap?"

"Yes. One of my Superintendent's bright ideas. He doesn't believe that Geoffrey was at the factory all that evening. He thinks he drove down into the town and collected Anne Winter. You know the traffic moves slowly because of the crowds. Someone is quite likely to have seen the Bentley and remembered it. And it's amazing what a response we get sometimes to one of those police notices. If Geoffrey isn't telling the truth about being at his office all the time, and if he went into the town at all, the chances are that Longton will catch up on him."

Rosalind fixed her eyes on her brother.

"And then?"

"He'll pull him in."

"He couldn't!"

"He will. And I'm afraid I don't think Geoffrey is telling the whole of the truth, either. I don't think he is the murderer, but he has some explaining to do. Roz, can't you make him come clean? He can't fight Longton. His only hope is to tell all the truth, and quick. Was he at the factory that night?"

Rosalind sighed.

"I don't know," she admitted, "I phoned him there, but there was no reply. But he could easily have told the switchboard not to leave him connected with an outside line. He wouldn't want interruptions when he was busy. I even rang David's flat, to see if he was there, but there was no reply from there either."

Barry looked up sharply.

"What was that? Did you say you phoned Kindersley that night?"

CHAPTER 13

THERE must be someone, thought Rosalind desperately, someone whom I can talk to, who can tell me the truth of what happened seventeen years ago. Mrs Winter, perhaps, might know, but she could not invade the stricken household with what would appear to be merely vulgar curiosity. Then she remembered that Mrs Winter herself had admitted that Anne had not confided in her. She would only know the story from her own angle.

Mrs Wareham, then? But no, she was Geoffrey's mother and life would have to go on after all this was over. She might misinterpret Rosalind's motives and it could lie between them for the rest of their lives.

Glenda? No, she was too young at the time, even if Rosalind could bring herself to approach her. The same was true of Giles. And the Colonel was not a man to whom she could explain herself.

Her brother's visit had left her full of forebodings. Fear for Geoffrey, with Superintendent Longton's shadow across his path. And fear for David, too, whom she liked and respected. But if he had killed Anne, he must be exposed, otherwise Geoffrey would suffer. And for Geoffrey, Rosalind would cheerfully have given her own life. If it were not for Geoffrey, she would try to protect David, although it was almost certainly too late. Her chance remark about the phone call had sent Barry tearing back into Broadgate.

But perhaps David would offer a reasonable explanation, and Geoffrey would remain the chief suspect. She could not sit still in Parrington and wait for her husband to be arrested.

She was not even thinking of Richard Seldon. She concentrated on Anne. Explain that murder, she reasoned, and the other will fall into place. And it all came back to what happened all those years ago.

Peter. Peter Maynard. He could tell her, surely. He was living with Geoffrey's family, and he was seventeen, old enough to be curious about what was going on, and undoubtedly finding out a great deal more than his elders intended him to know. He might even know more about Anne herself than the others, for there cannot have been more than a few months' difference in their ages. She wondered why she hadn't thought of asking him before. Cooped up in the house, as he was with his cold at the moment, he might not have realised that the police could do with his information.

In a brief mood of hope, Rosalind drove into Broadgate, to Peter's flat. She found Barry on the steps outside the modern block, arguing with the caretaker's wife. Mrs Jones was a thin, perpetually worried little woman, fussy to a degree and with a heart of gold. She had taken Peter Maynard to her scrawny bosom from the moment that he had moved into the newly-built flat, the substitute for the son she had never borne.

"I don't know what you want to keep worrying him for," she was complaining, "he's poorly enough without the police bothering him. And he won't call the doctor, silly boy," she added lovingly.

"I'm sorry," Barry replied patiently, "but I really must see him. Now, Mrs Jones, are you going to let me in or do I have to get him out of his bed to open the door?"

"I suppose I'll have to take you up there," she said reluctantly. Then she caught sight of Rosalind. "Oh, is that you, Mrs Lennard? The police are wanting to see poor Mr Maynard again. Not right, it isn't."

Rosalind joined the arguing pair on the steps.

"I'm sure Sergeant Thornley won't bother him more than absolutely necessary, Mrs Jones. But two murders have been committed. He's only doing his job. And I wanted to see Mr Maynard myself."

"You're different," muttered Mrs Jones, "he'll be glad to see you. Cheer him up a bit. That young woman of his hasn't been to see him once," she added jealously.

"Her father won't let her. He's a bit of a fanatic about colds. I expect she has phoned him."

Mrs Jones was not mollified.

"And dragging him up out of his bed to answer it, I

don't doubt. No consideration. Perhaps you'd persuade him to let me call the doctor, Mrs Lennard. Colds can hang on miserably at this time of the year. I told him that from the first, when the cold came up, yesterday week. But he wouldn't even go to bed with it then."

Barry and Rosalind made their escape from Mrs Jones, who eventually agreed to hand over Peter's key to Rosalind. Her manner implied that she would never have given it to Barry, not if he were five times a police officer.

"Bit of a tartar, that woman," he commented, as the lift took them up to the fourth floor. "Devoted to Maynard. And she gives him a pretty sound alibi for the night of Anne Winter's murder. Swears she gave him a hot toddy and a sleeping pill at eight o'clock. What a combination! Enough to knock a horse out, I should think. And she says he was sleeping peacefully when she looked in on him at ten. Add to that the fact that his car was locked up in its garage and her husband still had the keys, and he's out of it. And much the same story for last night," he went on, as they left the lift and walked along the corridor to Peter's flat, "but I'll have to see him, for form's sake, to satisfy the Old Man."

Peter's flat was the end one. Near the front door was a glass door to the fire escape. Barry peered through it, out over the complex of gardens at the rear of the flats.

"I suppose he could have knocked off Seldon," Barry said dubiously. "The house is over there. You can just see the chimneys through those trees. But not with the watchful Mrs Jones popping in and out like a Jack-in-the-box."

Rosalind let them into the flat, calling out as she did so. A voice from the bedroom answered them.

"You go in first," she stood back for Barry to pass her.

He was not in the bedroom long.

"I'm going to see what he can tell me about Anne," she told him as he was leaving the flat. "It seems a vain hope but there is no one else I can ask."

Barry nodded.

"Let me know if he comes up with anything. Good luck, Roz."

Rosalind put her head round the bedroom door. Peter was propped up in bed on a pile of pillows. He brightened when he saw her.

"You're a sight for sore eyes, Rosalind. Come to visit the sick? Don't come too close or you might catch it."

She found herself a chair.

"I'm not worried. I don't often catch colds. But, seriously, Peter, this one's surely more than just a summer cold. Don't you think you should have the doctor?"

He grimaced.

"I haven't much time for doctors. If I'd taken Ma Jones's advice and gone to bed in the first place, I would be over it by now. Not that I'm going to admit it to her. She's a bit of a tyrant."

"She's putting herself out, nursing you, you ungrateful creature," Rosalind retorted.

Peter had the grace to look ashamed.

"She's a decent old stick," he admitted, "but she insists on dosing me with some foul concoction of her own. Last night I just had time to phone Lucille before it hit me. Which is just as well, as it turns out. Seems by the timing it stops the coppers thinking I finished off poor old Richard."

Rosalind left her chair and wandered to the window. She hadn't come to hear about Peter's alibis. She wanted to talk about Anne, but it was difficult to steer the conversation round.

"Here, mind my plant," said Peter. "That's my prize specimen."

Rosalind glanced down. Intent on her own problem, she had not noticed that she was almost leaning on a flourishing primula in a pot on the window-sill.

"Oh, I'm sorry."

She moved back quickly, steadying the plant with her hand. Peter was right to be proud of it. The pinky tones of the large flower heads toned with the pastel shades of the room. It occurred to her that there was more to Peter than met the eye. He might be a brilliant salesman and mad about boats, but somewhere an artist lurked. The whole flat, now she thought of it, was decorated in unerring taste and she knew that Peter himself had planned the lot.

She decided on a bold approach.

"Peter, Geoffrey's in trouble. That Superintendent thinks he killed Anne."

"Nonsense," scoffed Peter. "Why should he?"

"I don't know. I can't imagine how the official police mind works. But you can take it from me that he is trying to gather evidence against Geoffrey. And we've got to stop him."

"But what can we do?"

"It all comes back to the events which led to Anne Winter's leaving home, and breaking her engagement. In other words, we must find out who was the father of her child. He's the only person who could have a motive for killing her now. Who else would have any reason to want poor Anne out of the way?"

"But, Roz, it was seventeen years ago. Whoever it was has kept his secret all this time, and if Anne was murdered for that reason, he has also killed to cover it up. What can we hope to discover now?"

"Peter, you were there at the time."

"No one told me anything. I wasn't supposed to know."

"I bet you did, all the same."

She surprised a grin out of him.

"For heaven's sake, Peter," she went on, "don't hold back. If everyone who knew anything about it at all pooled their information, I'm sure the truth would come out at once. But so many people have a bit of the truth that no one can recognise it. Geoffrey didn't get Anne pregnant. If he had, he would never have cast her and the child off. Peter, you must have had some suspicions."

"Well," he began, then stopped.

The indecision on his face spurred Rosalind on.

"Was it David?"

Peter relaxed, but he could not meet her eyes.

"I thought so. At the time," he admitted.

*   *   *

Superintendent Longton looked up from a pile of papers as his sergeant came into the room.

"Ah, there you are. What have you got?"

Barry dropped into his own chair. He had had a long and tiring day, and it was by no means finished yet.

"I've seen all Seldon's brother-directors, sir. Nothing outstanding, at the first look. Hardwick says he was at home, and his wife backs him up, but then, she would. Threadwell was at a dinner party. That one should be easy enough. Colonel Winter was at home, too, with his wife and son, but they were scattered all over that house, so they can't really vouch for each other. There's an interesting thing there. The Colonel simply won't listen to a word about Fenella Winter. He's trying to pretend she doesn't exist. Giles, the son, on the other hand, is obviously anxious lest he should have to share part of his inheritance with his unwanted niece. The mother wants to know about the girl, keeps on repeating that it will be impossible for them to have her there with them, but once she sets eyes on her, I reckon she'll want her, all right."

"Huh," grunted Longton, "did they ask you where she was?"

"Only Mrs Winter."

"I hope you didn't tell her."

"I said she was with friends in London. That's as much as I said to any of them."

"We have enough on our hands without having to set a guard on her. If her father killed her mother to prevent himself being exposed, he might well have a go at the girl, too, in case she knows his identity."

"Which she doesn't."

"He may not know that. So don't tell them. Any of them. All right, go on."

"Maynard was the nearest to Seldon, geographically speaking, and you could nip down the fire escape outside his flat and across the gardens to Seldon's place. He would know the lay-out, too, since he keeps his boat there. But he was being dosed by the caretaker's wife at ten to eight, and chatting to his girl friend on the phone at a quarter-past."

"That's pretty well the limits on Seldon," growled Longton. "I've the results of the autopsy here. Seldon had a meal at about six—char confirms that, she stayed to make his tea—so he could get to the hospital to see his wife. The doc reckons, from the state of the stomach, that he was dead before nine o'clock, but for choice a bit earlier. We know he came home just before eight. If Lennard killed him, it was round a quarter-past, when his car was seen there. And if he didn't, Seldon didn't answer the door to him because he was dead already. So there you are."

"Which leaves Kindersley," said Barry, "and he says he was at home, with no one to prove or disprove it."

"Like last time."

"Only," said Barry softly, "last time he was lying."

Longton sat up.

"What's that?"

"He wasn't telling the truth, sir. My sister tried to phone him that evening, and there was no reply from his number."

"Indeed? I want a word with him."

Barry grinned.

"I thought you would, sir. He's waiting outside."

Longton favoured him with a long stare.

"All right, sergeant," he said, with a hint of menace in his voice to warn Barry that not one tiny detail of this would be forgotten, "wheel him in."

The Superintendent watched in silence as David was brought in and sat down in a chair facing his desk. The man looked exhausted, but there was an air of dogged resolution about him. Not an easy nut to crack, thought Longton, but with the pressure applied at the right place. . . .

"There is a discrepancy in your first statement, Mr Kindersley," he began.

"I wish to make a new statement," David cut in.

Longton nodded to Barry, who was poised, pencil in hand, over his notebook.

"Very well."

"I didn't tell you the truth. Last Wednesday, I did not spend the whole of the evening alone in my flat. I went out."

"Where did you go?"

"Into the town."

Longton's gaze travelled over his witness.

"A man called at 'The Ship', the hotel where Miss Winter was staying. He called twice that evening. I should like you to take part in an identity parade, Mr Kindersley."

"There is no need," said David, "I was that man."

"Tell me about it," invited Longton. "Take your time. But first I should warn you that what you say will be taken down and may be used in evidence."

"I realise that. But I didn't kill her. I didn't even see her. I wanted to. Geoffrey told me that afternoon that she was back and staying at 'The Ship'. I thought about nothing else for the rest of the day. When I got home, I decided I would go and see her. So I went along to the hotel. But she was out. I hung around the place for a bit, then went back again, but she was still out. I wandered round the town a bit more, then it occurred to me that perhaps she had gone out to Parrington to see her people, and I had better take my place in the queue. So I went home."

"What time was all this?"

David shrugged.

"I don't know. I was a bit confused, with the excitement of her coming back after all these years. I didn't notice the time. It must have been after ten when I went home."

Longton sighed.

"And I suppose you saw no one that you knew?"

"I doubt if I would have noticed my best friend that evening unless I had bumped into him," said David frankly.

" 'The Ship' has a telephone. Did you phone Miss Winter there during the afternoon?"

"No."

"It would have been the logical thing to do."

"I never even thought of it, Superintendent."

"You didn't make an appointment to meet her later that evening, say, after the cinemas had closed?"

David stared at him.

"Cinemas?" he echoed.

"Miss Winter went to the cinema that evening," Longton explained, "presumably to kill time before an appointment which she had made over the telephone earlier in the day. I am asking you, did you make that appointment?"

"I told you, I didn't speak to her on the phone. And if I had an appointment with her, why would I have bothered going to the hotel, and twice at that?"

"To create an impression of innocence, Mr Kindersley."

David's fair complexion flushed.

"I didn't kill her. Good God! Superintendent, can't you understand what I am trying to tell you? There has only ever been one woman for me and she was Anne Winter. I loved her. I have loved her all through these years. Can't you understand what it meant to me that she had come back? Geoffrey is married, so I wouldn't be trying to cut him out. When we were students, I had nothing to offer her. He had everything. But I knew she didn't love him. Not that she had told me. She never so much as glanced at me."

"Were you the father of her child?"

David choked back the sudden and unaccustomed tears.

"If I had been," he cried, "I would never have disowned her or the child. I would have been proud to say they were mine."

There was a silence, while Longton waited for the man to regain his composure.

"Mr Kindersley," he said at last, "this is all very interesting, but, if you didn't see Anne Winter that night, why didn't you tell us all this in the first place? You made a statement, and on your own admission it was false. Why?"

"I don't know. I was shocked by the news of her death. I just don't know, Superintendent."

"You must have known that we would find out about a man calling twice at the hotel, looking for Miss Winter."

"I—I didn't think."

"At the least, you are responsible for the waste of a good deal of our time, chasing after an identification of that man. But I suggest to you that you would never have told us the truth had it not been for Sergeant Thornley managing to disprove your original story. That is not the action of an innocent citizen, Kindersley. I am not satisfied with your new statement, and I am afraid that you will have to remain here for a while. If there is anything you wish to add to that statement," he ended invitingly, "now is the time to do it."

CHAPTER 14

As the day wore on and no disaster overwhelmed them, Rosalind regained her confidence. Geoffrey was still preoccupied with his private worries, but she knew from the odd hints which he dropped that these were concerning the factory rather than the murders. For once she did not mind him fretting over the wretched information leak. It kept his mind off other things. All the same, she tried to cheer him up with an account of Peter and Mrs Jones, the domestic tyrant.

Geoffrey grinned.

"Peter has always prided himself with his way with females. He's overdone it a bit this time. You know, I thought he would never settle down. I've lost count of the number of girls he's had, all of them pretty glamorous pieces, too. But from the moment he met Lucille Threadwell, he gave them up."

"Perhaps Mrs Jones paved the way," suggested Rosalind lightly, "making him appreciate being looked after."

"Or maybe he thought getting married was the only escape from her," chimed in Geoffrey.

Rosalind found she was able to laugh freely. She stretched out luxuriously in her deckchair, placed carefully in the middle of the newly laid lawn, to catch all the sun. Geoffrey lay on the grass beside her.

Sally came running up to demand if they could go to the beach later in the afternoon.

Rosalind glanced up. In the west, a few darkish clouds were gathering.

"If it doesn't rain," she promised.

"Peter has a domestic streak," Rosalind picked up the thread of their idle conversation. "Look how well he has decorated the flat."

"True," agreed Geoffrey, vaguely, his eyes fixed on the figure of Sally racing round at the bottom of the garden in the wild uncleared jungle.

In a moment, thought Rosalind, he'll get up and go down there to her.

"Even to the flowers," she went on, unwilling to let him go even to Sally for a few moments more. "He had a primula on his bedroom window-sill, a lovely pinky colour. You couldn't have found anything which went better with the rest of the room."

Geoffrey swung himself into a sitting position.

"What's that? A primula? Peter?"

"Yes. Why not?"

"You must be mistaken. Peter would never have a primula, especially in his bedroom."

"Darling, I know a primula. And why shouldn't he?"

"He daren't go near the things. He has an allergy. When he was a kid we used to wonder why he always had such a cold in summer. Then, we tracked it down to the primulas. Mother was very fond of them, and there were lots in the garden. And in the house. One sniff of those things, and—" he broke off, staring at his wife. "Well, the young devil! Of all the nerve! I've a good mind to get a box of those tablets—what are they? Anti-histamine, I think. Anyway, they cure allergies—and take it over to him."

"You don't mean he's *faked* that cold?"

Geoffrey was torn between amusement and vexation.

"I mean just that."

"But why?"

"To dodge the board meeting, of course. Old Thread-well's a bit of a hypochondriac. He'd have a fit if anyone expected him to go near someone with a streaming cold."

"No wonder Peter won't let Mrs Jones send for the doctor."

"You have to hand it to him," said Geoffrey with reluctant admiration, "he worked it out jolly well. This so-called cold of his came up over a week ago. I think it was the Friday. And he ascribed it to the wetting he had had when he was out sailing on Tuesday evening. No doubt he arranged that, too; it would all be part of the plan. Wetting on Tuesday, three days' incubation and then the cold on Friday. And all well in advance of the meeting. Then he went into his routine of 'I can't go sick, I'm too busy,' until he was so bad that I sent him home. And on the Wednesday, of course. Just right for the meeting the following day. It must have come as a bit of a shock when the thing was postponed."

"He'd have to have another sniff of his primula," giggled Rosalind. "I suppose that is why he couldn't throw it out. He didn't know how long he was going to need it."

"He doesn't need it any more," said Geoffrey grimly.

"Oh, no, don't spoil it," pleaded Rosalind. "Think how he has suffered for it. All those ghastly knock-out potions Mrs Jones has brewed up for him. And, Geoffrey," she added seriously, "if Peter has been malingering, he has done it for your sake. He doesn't want to have to support Threadwell against you. He doesn't want to choose between you and Lucille."

Geoffrey was on his feet, looking down at her.

"If I can't win by fair means, I won't do it by foul."

"Threadwell doesn't fight fair."

"But I'm not Threadwell, Roz. No, Peter will be at that board meeting tomorrow if I have to fetch him myself—and dose him with pills till he rattles. Come to think of it, someone will have to fetch him. On Friday, Threadwell insisted on sending him home in his own car. Peter's is still at the factory. I'll give David a ring and ask him to do it."

A cloud blotted out the sun.

Geoffrey's face was turned away from her, but his whole body was stilled, as though the name had put a spell on him.

David, thought Rosalind.

It was like the touch of a dead man's hand on her warm flesh.

*   *   *

Sunday dawned bright and sunny. Rosalind woke from a heavy and unrefreshing sleep to hear Sally's clear voice from the garden below her window. Then an answering voice, deeper, just as familiar and loved. And the sound of a ball and another squeal of delight from the child.

She dragged herself out of bed and over to the window. Sally and Geoffrey were throwing a large red ball to each other. She watched them for a moment. They were absorbed in their game, warmed by the morning sun, carefree.

Geoffrey appeared carefree only for the sake of the child, she knew.

Rosalind shivered and reached for her dressing-gown to protect her from the chill which had nothing to do with the weather.

A quarter of an hour later, washed, dressed and braced—she hoped—to meet whatever horrors the day had in store for them, she went downstairs. She found her family in the kitchen, preparing breakfast, with much laughter.

"We thought you were still asleep," Geoffrey hailed her from the stove, where he was making toast.

"You should have waited for your cup of tea," Sally reproved her. "We were going to bring it up in a minute."

Geoffrey had quitted his post.

"Cheer up, darling," he said, lifting her off her feet and giving her a smacking kiss.

"Geoffrey, you idiot, put me down. The toast!"

He dropped her and dashed over to the stove.

"Too late," he announced, fishing the burnt remnants from under the grill, while acrid fumes filled the kitchen.

"I'll give it to the birds," called Sally, reaching for it.

"Mind, it's hot."

But the child had grabbed the plate and was already out in the garden.

"Oh, Geoffrey!" exclaimed Rosalind, nearer to tears than laughter.

The smile faded from his face, revealing the lines of strain and sleeplessness.

"Roz," he said uncertainly, and they fell into each other's arms and clung together.

Sally returned. The moment passed.

Later that morning, Rosalind burst out, "Geoffrey, surely there is something we can do!"

It was like continuing a conversation which had been broken off by a momentary interruption.

He did not pretend to misunderstand.

"I don't see that there is," he replied sombrely. "I didn't kill Anne and I didn't kill Richard. How I convince the police is another matter. There's one thing, though. There can't be more than circumstantial evidence against me. Anything else doesn't exist. What we have to do is keep our heads."

"They are trying to catch you in a lie," said Rosalind slowly. "I don't quite understand it, but Superintendent Longton thinks he can find someone who saw your car in Broadgate the night Anne was killed. Away from the factory, that is."

"That bit on the wireless," he muttered. "But there wasn't an accident."

"No, but it may still work. A near-miss, or an emergency stop in the crowded streets near the front. Geoffrey, they know you aren't telling all the truth about that night. I know it, too. You're not a good liar, my darling."

Geoffrey stared at her, aghast.

"Is it as obvious as all that?"

"I'm afraid it is. Where did you go that night?"

He ran his hand through his hair.

"Well, it's true enough that I was at the factory most of the time. I didn't leave my office until past eleven. But I did go into the town earlier. About six o'clock. I wasn't there long."

"You went to see Anne?"

"That was the idea. I had phoned her after I spoke to her father. I had to tell her that he wouldn't even listen. She took it very well. But then, she would. She would never have let anyone know how much it hurt her. She and her father were a lot alike, and they both had too much pride. That's why they hurt each other so much. I asked her how long she was staying in Broadgate. She said she had a week's holiday and she might as well spend it here. It would be the last time she would see the place. So I told her not to give up hope. I would have another go at him and speak to her mother, too. She said she didn't want me to, but I told her not to be silly."

"And what did she say to that?"

Geoffrey pulled a face.

"She told me I hadn't changed. Am I really dictatorial, Roz? Oh, well, never mind that now. Later, I thought it might be better if I had a word with her, so I drove over to her hotel. That is, I set out for it, but I never reached it. Because I saw Anne herself, walking through the crowds down by the Clock Tower. Of course, I tried to park, but there wasn't an inch, and by the time I found a place, and retraced my steps, she had disappeared. I hung around for a few minutes, but she was going away from the hotel, and there was no sign of her. So I packed it in, and went back to the office. That's all there is to it."

"But, darling, why didn't you tell the police?"

"I don't really know," he admitted sheepishly. "It was stupid of me. I suppose I didn't want to be involved. After all, it wouldn't help them at all. I don't know where she was going. She was alone. I didn't get the chance of a word with her. And it seemed so easy. They seemed to take my story so well the first time."

"And have not believed a word you have said to them since," commented Rosalind bitterly. "Geoffrey, what is it going to sound like now, telling them?"

"I'm not going to, unless I can help it. You don't have

to underline it, Roz. I've put myself in an impossible position."

"No," replied Rosalind quickly, "better to tell them now. I agree it will look bad, but it will be worse if they face you with some sort of evidence. Geoffrey, don't be a fool."

He smiled at her lovingly, but shook his head.

"No, darling, they would never believe me. I'm in a big enough mess. Don't let's make it any worse."

CHAPTER 15

"Look at them," muttered Superintendent Longton sourly, as Barry drove him along the front at Broadgate, "enjoying themselves."

He made it sound like the deadliest of the sins.

Barry glanced down at the beach. It was already crowded, and the sea was full of bathers.

"Baking themselves in the sun," Longton went on resentfully, "while we have to work. Do you realise, Sergeant, that I haven't had a full day in my garden for over a month. Weeds all over the place. And it's nothing to laugh at, either, my lad. Did you know I used to win prizes with my dahlias?"

"No, sir," replied Barry, keeping his face straight.

"Fat lot of prizes I'd win now. The booby perhaps, if they had such things at flower shows. Anyway," he added with great satisfaction, "they might as well enjoy themselves while they can. There will be a storm later on, you mark my words."

He could be right at that, thought Barry. There is a sultriness in the air. You can feel it building up.

"I wonder how Kindersley feels this morning?" he ventured.

"Damned thankful he didn't spend the night in the cells, if he knows what's what," replied Longton. "I don't blame you for fixing on him, Thornley; he's as good a suspect as any. With a fishy story, if you like, and nothing to speak of as an alibi. But, there isn't a trace of Anne Winter in his car, not so much as a hair or half a fingerprint. Nor did he hire or borrow someone else's to take her out to Parrington."

"As far as we can make out," Barry reminded him.

"And it is difficult to see from the timing of Lennard's call, which they both admit, how he could have killed Seldon. Not that that is conclusive. I suppose there might be a way round that, since he's clever. No, it's my guess he's clean, but there is always the chance I could be wrong," he said with the confidence of one who can't remember the last time that happened to him, it was so long ago.

It jarred on Barry, reminding him of the precariousness of his own position, now that he had dared to voice opposition to the Superintendent.

He pulled into the car park at the back of the police station.

"Here we are, sir," he said cheerfully.

Longton grinned at him, knowingly.

The sight of a desk piled high with reports wiped the smile off his face.

"Better get started," he said.

They worked in silence for a while.

"Well. Well. Well," said Longton, a little later. "Here's another bit of interesting evidence. A note from Seldon's lawyer, about his Will. Everything goes to his wife, with the exception of his holding of shares in Lennard Plastics. And that goes to his god-son, Geoffrey Lennard, with the proviso that the income is paid to Mrs Seldon during her lifetime. Not a bad little inheritance for someone who is fighting to retain control of his company. How do you like that?"

Barry didn't like it at all.

There was a knock on the door, and a uniformed

constable informed them that a man was outside, in
response to the appeal on the wireless.

Longton's smile broadened.

"Bring him in."

Barry had to admit that Geoffrey's prospects were
growing blacker. The new witness, a holidaymaker, who
had been driving his car peacefully along the front, one
of a line of slowly moving traffic, was full of righteous
indignation about the man in the Bentley who had so
nearly caused an accident.

"Right in front of the Clock Tower, it was, Superintendent. Stopped just like that, looking at some woman,
as far as I could make out. If we hadn't been crawling,
I'd have been in his boot, and then there'd have been
a rumpus, him with a great big car and all. I don't know
if that's of any use to you, Superintendent, but if it's that
same Bentley you're after, I hope you throw the book
at him. Proper menace, he is."

Longton assured him that his public-spirited assistance
was highly appreciated.

"Observant, too," said Longton triumphantly, when
the man had departed. "You couldn't have a better description of Lennard or of his car."

"Little perisher," muttered Barry under his breath. As
far as he was concerned, the insult applied equally to the
witness and his superintendent.

"It will be interesting to hear Geoffrey Lennard explain that one away," observed Longton, picking up
another paper. "What's this. Oh, Ealing." He read it
through quickly. "Blast. Not a trace of the Bentley or
another car. That street, where the Winters' flat is, is a
quiet one at night. You would have thought someone
would have heard something. Only some woman who
lives opposite who was woken by a motor-bike starting
up. That's a fat lot of use. Not one of those people owns
a motor-bike. Oh, well, this is where we begin again.
We'll have to check all the garages for motor-bikes. After

all," he added thoughtfully, "Winter could have ridden out to Parrington on a pillion."

Another knock heralded the constable from the inquiry desk.

"There's a woman here, sir. Wants to see you. She says she recognised the picture of the dead woman which appeared in yesterday's papers."

She was a small nervous woman, whose every movement seemed an effort. She sank thankfully into the chair which Barry pushed forward for her.

"Now then, Miss . . . er. Mrs . . . er," began Longton.

"Miss," she informed him, "Miss Aileen Stokes. It's about that picture. Are you the Scotland Yard man?"

"Yes. I'm Superintendent Longton. You saw the picture in yesterday's paper?"

Miss Stokes nodded eagerly.

"I knew her at once. I'd have come in yesterday, only I was on the late shift, and I was that tired when I got home. I'm always tired," she added sadly.

"Now take your time, and tell it your own way," Longton said kindly. "You recognised the picture. Where had you seen her?"

"Why, at the Winter Garden, of course. I'm a waitress in the restaurant there."

"So. You saw Anne Winter in the restaurant."

"Yes, poor thing. Of course, in the season it's terrible, we're so rushed off our feet, we'd never notice who was there, only if they had two heads or something, as I always say," she went on with a sad little smile which vanished guiltily the moment she perceived that her stock joke aroused no response in either of the detectives. "Oh, dear, have I said something wrong?"

"Indeed you have not, Miss Stokes. In fact, I think you are going to prove a most valuable witness. Do I understand that you saw this woman during the winter months?"

"Yes, that's what I'm telling you. It was in January.

I know that because I'd been off sick for a couple of days and it was my first day back."

"Yes. Go on. You are sure it was this same woman?"

"I don't suppose I would have taken much notice of her, in the ordinary way," she admitted, "but I'm good at faces, once I take an interest in people. I can remember faces if I don't see their owners for years," she told him proudly.

"And what aroused your interest in Anne Winter?"

"Well," the little waitress was a thought self-conscious, "it was because of who she was with, if you follow me."

Longton's face was grim.

"I follow you, Miss Stokes, and I don't blame you for taking notice of a handsome man. Tall and dark, was he?"

"Oh, no, you've got it all wrong, sir. It wasn't a *man*. It was a girl. I don't think I have ever seen anyone so beautiful," she said simply. "Not even on the films."

"Can you describe this girl, Miss Stokes?"

"Well, she was fair, real silky blonde hair, and a gorgeous figure. I've seen her once or twice since. She lives somewhere round here. I've seen her driving a white car."

Longton flashed a glance at Barry, who nodded.

There was only one person who fitted that description. Glenda Hardwick.

*   *   *

Edna Purvis took her time washing up after Sunday dinner. Not that she could afford to dawdle. She had to catch the two o'clock bus into Broadgate, to be at the hospital for visiting time. Even so, she would not get the full two hours, but there was no other bus she could catch. And she couldn't expect Purvis to take her in on the back of his motor-bike. She had long since given up expecting Purvis to put himself out for her or anyone else.

Her youngest grandchild was rolling about on the narrow strip of garden at the back of the cottage. For a moment, she let herself watch him. But the respite could not last for ever. She must make up her own mind. No one else could do it for her.

If only she could bring herself to speak to Mrs Lennard. There was a girl she felt she could trust. There was a stability, a sanity about Rosalind Lennard which appealed to Mrs Purvis. Basically, they spoke the same language.

But village gossip had it that Geoffrey Lennard had killed Miss Anne. True enough, the police had called at the converted barn several times. Not that Mrs Purvis believed that Geoffrey was the murderer. It didn't ring true to her, but she admitted to herself that, after all, she hardly knew him. Years ago, she had only seen him through Miss Anne's eyes. Now she looked at him through Rosalind's. She was just being sentimental about Geoffrey Lennard, because she didn't want to see Rosalind and that lovely child, Sally, hurt.

This won't do, Edna Purvis, she admonished herself. You'll miss that bus. Purvis's mother might be paralysed from the stroke and scarcely able to speak, but she was still "all there" in the head. She knew exactly what time she could expect her daughter-in-law to arrive. . . .

The bustle of the last-minute rush for the bus kept her mind off the problem for a while, but as soon as she was settled in her seat and the bus was passing through the deserted lanes, it came back to her. And at the back of the almost-empty vehicle, the conductor was discussing the case with another passenger.

"Them sort of people," he was saying, "they'd do anything to hush things up."

"Ah," agreed the passenger, knowledgeably, "I reckon it's the father of the child as killed her. And that other fellow. Bound to be the same murderer. Couldn't have two of them running round here together."

But you're wrong, thought Mrs Purvis, you are all wrong. The police are wrong.

That checked her. She had a great faith in the ability of the police. Surely they had found out by now that the father of Anne's child couldn't possibly have killed her? Not that she was entirely certain herself who he was, but she had her suspicions.

The conductor and his friend had abandoned the subject of murder.

"Going to be a storm, I shouldn't wonder," the passenger remarked.

"Wet all them trippers on the sands," agreed the conductor with satisfaction. "You want next stop, Ma?" he called down the bus. "Nearest to the hospital."

Mrs Purvis heaved her sturdy body out of the seat. She felt very tired, which was unusual for her. It's all this worry, she thought, why should it depend on me to put the police off the wrong track they are following?

A new thought struck her. Maybe the police knew all about it, had been told the truth about Anne Winter's baby, and were keeping it quiet to lull the real murderer into a sense of security.

All very well for a play on the telly, she told herself, as she left the bus and plodded the hundred yards down a side turning to reach the hospital, but not in real life.

The least she could do, to satisfy herself, was check up.

CHAPTER 16

GLENDA HARDWICK flashed a glance of pure scorn at Superintendent Longton, then turned her head away and stared out of the window. It wasn't an inspiring view, for Longton's room in Broadgate police station looked out on a patch of tarmac and a high brick wall. Apparently Glenda preferred it to the faces of the two Scotland Yard detectives. Her elegantly shod foot tapped impatiently.

She's too damn stupid to realise that she is caught, thought Longton savagely. This has gone beyond the stage where outraged denials could do any good. If her husband were here, he'd see that quickly enough. Not that it would help us much. Hardwick is the type to tell her to shut up until their solicitor was present. No, on balance, it was just as well that Hardwick was out when they picked her up.

"Well, Mrs Hardwick?" he prompted her balefully.

Glenda's eyes flickered over him briefly before returning to the brick wall.

"I've nothing more to say. The whole thing is totally ridiculous. I don't believe that a waitress can remember people like that. Anyway, she couldn't have done. I didn't even know Anne Winter. I hadn't seen her since I was seven."

"She picked you out from a line-up."

It had livened up the Sunday morning at the station. The young constables had raised no objection to finding a few lovelies to range alongside Glenda Hardwick. Little Miss Stokes had been quite positive in her identification. There had not been a moment's hesitation.

"You told her who I was beforehand," Glenda flung at him.

Longton kept his temper with an effort. He would have liked to put this spoilt beauty across his knee and spank her.

"That is not true, Mrs Hardwick," he replied coldly. "Do you deny that you have visited the restaurant at the Winter Garden?"

"No, of course not. It's one of the only places open out of the season. That's why your girl identified me. I do go there, especially in the winter. But not with Anne. She is mistaken there."

"So when she saw you there in January, you claim that you were with someone else? Which of your friends resembles Anne Winter?"

Glenda bit her lip.

"How should I remember who I was with that day?"

"That wasn't what I asked you, Mrs Hardwick."

"I could have been with anyone," said Glenda defiantly.

"So you couldn't say which of your friends might be mistaken for Miss Winter? None of them. That's the truth, isn't it?"

"I really don't know," she replied, affecting boredom. She consulted her wrist-watch, pointedly. "It's past two o'clock. I want to go home to my lunch. You can't keep me here for ever."

"I'll keep you here until I am satisfied with your statement," Longton retorted. "We haven't had any lunch either. It will be sent in shortly."

There was the first hint of a crack in Glenda's composure.

"I want to see my husband," she declared.

"We have not been able to contact him. There is a message waiting for him at your house."

"I don't believe you. He must be home by now. He only went over to see Mr Threadwell for a little while."

"We phoned Mr Threadwell's house," Longton explained patiently. "Miss Threadwell says her father and your husband have gone out for a drink. And she doesn't know where. Now, Mrs Hardwick, the sooner you tell me the truth, the sooner you will be going home. We have wasted a lot of time already. Now——" he broke off as a knock sounded at the door. "See who that is, will you, Sergeant?"

Obediently, Barry opened the door. A constable stood there, a thin clip of papers in his hand. Barry took it and thanked him. He laid it on Longton's desk.

There was a snapshot, a couple of sheets of fingerprints, and a scribbled note from Superintendent Marsh.

Barry glanced at Glenda. Her eyes were fixed on the photograph. Her face had suddenly gone pale.

Longton looked up.

"Mrs Hardwick," he began and his voice was hard, "this photograph was found in a handbag belonging to the dead woman. We know it was in her possession before she came to Broadgate last Tuesday. It is of your brother, Mr Geoffrey Lennard, and it was taken by your mother sometime last year. How do you account for the fact that your fingerprints are on it?"

Glenda stared at him. She moistened her lips.

"We have been trying to establish how it came into the possession of Anne Winter," Longton went on. "I suggest that you gave it to her, when you saw her in January of this year."

Still Glenda did not reply.

"So far," pursued Longton, in a silky voice, "you are the first person whom we have discovered to be in contact with Anne Winter before her second visit to Broadgate. Sergeant Thornley, kindly pass me Mrs Hardwick's statement of her movements on the night of the first murder."

Silently, Barry sorted it out from the now bulging file, and handed it to him. Glenda watched them both, petrified.

"Ah yes," said Longton, "you were at home with your husband. Sergeant, we will put out a call for Edward Hardwick. We had better pull him in. At the least he will be an accessory."

Glenda found her voice.

"What do you mean, an accessory?" she faltered.

"To murder, Mrs Hardwick. Let me remind you that a conviction for murder carries with it a long prison sentence. You would not be very beautiful after serving a life sentence," he added cruelly.

Glenda was shaking.

"You can't think I killed Anne!"

"Why not?" returned Longton calmly, and watched while panic overwhelmed her.

"Hysterics," he remarked dispassionately, over the

noise which now came from Glenda's lovely mouth. "Call one of the women out there, Sergeant. She'll talk when she has calmed down."

A policewoman came in, to deal with Glenda. Ten minutes later, Glenda, her eyes swollen with tears and her face streaked with wrecked make-up, faced Longton again.

"I'll tell you," she said sullenly, "but I didn't have anything to do with the murder."

Longton made no comment. He cautioned her and nodded to Barry to start taking it all down.

"So it was Anne Winter who was with you in the Winter Garden in January?"

"Yes. That was the first time I had seen her since she went away."

"How did you meet her?"

"I had been shopping in the town. It was a nice day, sunny, so I went for a walk along the front. I sat down for a bit, in one of the shelters. This woman was there."

"And you got into conversation?" supplied Longton, as Glenda hesitated.

"I hadn't recognised her, but she knew me. She said she had seen my wedding photograph. In one of the magazines," she added with a touch of her old self. "Of course, as soon as she mentioned her name, I realised. So I took her to have some tea at the Winter Garden."

"Did she ask after her family? Or after your brother?"

Glenda shook her head.

"She didn't say anything about herself. Not after introducing herself."

"She didn't tell you that she was ill?"

"No. She didn't mention it."

"Did she say why she had come back?"

"No."

Longton sighed. It was painfully clear that Glenda Hardwick was not interested in anything or anyone except herself. Anne Winter could have dropped dead at her feet and Glenda would not have wanted to know why.

"All right, what about the photograph? If she hadn't asked after your brother, why did you give it to her?"

"But I didn't. Then, that is. I gave it to her later."

"So you knew where to find her?"

"I didn't know where she lived. But she had mentioned where she worked. I went in to see her when I was in Town."

"When was that?"

"The week before last. On the Friday."

There was a silence. Longton gazed at his witness, and Glenda stared back at him, naked fear on her face.

"So," he said, at last, "you went to London on the Friday and you visited Anne Winter at the shop where she worked. You gave her a photograph of your brother. Her former fiancé. We know that she made the decision to go to Broadgate again, that night, the Friday. She was killed the following Tuesday. Did you know you were luring her to her death?"

Glenda cowered in her chair.

"No, no, I didn't. I didn't."

"But you said something to her which made her decide to try her luck with her family. And with Geoffrey Lennard. What was it?"

Glenda had begun to cry again.

"Did you tell her your brother was married?"

She shook her head, speechlessly.

"So, in fact, you gave her Geoffrey Lennard's photograph and you told her that he had never married. What was the idea, Mrs Hardwick?"

"It isn't what you think," Glenda gasped, through her sobs. "I was only trying to help my husband. And it was nothing to do with the murder. I didn't know she was going to be killed. There's a row going on, at the factory, amongst the directors. Mr Threadwell wants to get Geoffrey voted out. He's going to put Edward in his place. Geoffrey keeps Edward down. He will never let him run things as he wants. I thought, if Anne reappeared, the week of the board meeting, it might . . . it might. . . ." Tears overwhelmed her voice.

"You thought it might put your brother off his stroke," Longton finished for her grimly, "so that he wouldn't be able to fight back so well. Very clever. And Anne Winter, poor fool, fell for it. If Geoffrey Lennard thought enough of her not to look at other women, there was a chance he would speak for her to her family. There might be a chance that he would marry her. It wouldn't have done her much good, but it would have secured the future for her daughter. Which was her main worry. What else have you to tell me, Mrs Hardwick? Were your husband and Mr Threadwell in on this scheme with you?"

Glenda burst into fresh tears.

"No. They didn't know anything about it."

"And what happened when Anne Winter found out that Geoffrey Lennard had a wife, after all?"

Glenda shivered at the memory.

"She phoned me. On Tuesday evening. Edward took the call," she said painfully. "He made me tell him what I had done. He was furious with me."

"Yet, not only did Anne Winter make another phone call to Lennard's house, but she also went out to dinner with him that night," said Longton thoughtfully. "She must have guessed by then that she had been had, and you had got her down here for some purpose of your own. But apparently, she was charitable enough not to tell Lennard what you had done. You didn't deserve that, Mrs Hardwick. Not that you could be sure of it. You might have thought it well worth getting rid of Anne Winter for good and all."

Glenda started to scream again.

*　　*　　*

Edward Hardwick had the rat's instinctive knowledge of the time to leave the sinking ship. Glenda's tomfoolery was bound to become common knowledge now. From every point of view, he must be known to have had nothing to do with it, no matter who triumphed in the tussle in the board room. If Geoffrey won through, after all, he would pitch him out immediately, if he suspected that Edward had played any part in the mean little scheme. And as for Stanley Threadwell, Edward had no illusions in that direction. There was only one gleam of hope, one possible advantage to be gained from the regrettable situation, and that was to play the chivalrous husband, keeping silent for the sake of his foolish little wife.

"My wife meant no harm, Superintendent," he said.

"That is as maybe," growled Longton.

"I had the truth out of her after Miss Winter had telephoned that day. The Tuesday, of course. And I made her promise that she would not see Miss Winter again. Her brother's marriage—and to a virtual stranger —had upset her, you understand."

"What you mean is, she had her eye on his money," said Longton bluntly.

Edward looked pained.

"She may not have liked seeing family property going to a woman we knew nothing about. And one with a child she got from somewhere," he added distastefully. "Not that I have anything against Mrs Rosalind Lennard personally, you understand, Superintendent, but naturally one has reservations when a member of the family marries outside the usual circle."

Barry regarded the end of Edward's pointed nose, at the spot where he longed to plant a power-packed bunched fist. But Scotland Yard discipline held good.

"If Mrs Lennard's antecedents satisfy us," Longton told Edward nastily, "I don't see why they shouldn't do for you, too. And if it is of any interest to you, we know about her first marriage. If you will take my advice, Mr Hardwick, you will not go spreading rumours about the legitimacy of her daughter. You might find yourself in a tricky position, one day."

Not half, thought Barry. Just you wait till this case is wrapped up and I can emerge as Rosalind's brother. It will be my pleasure to knock your pretty denture down your throat.

"Anyhow," Longton was saying, "all that is beside the point. We aren't discussing Lennard's wife. We are talking about yours. So you told her to keep away from Anne Winter. What then?"

"Nothing, Superintendent. The next thing we knew, Anne had been murdered. That is all I can tell you."

"Is it, indeed? Well let me inform you, Mr Hardwick, that it isn't nearly enough. Neither of you can produce a satisfactory account of your movements for the times of either of the murders. In your position, it isn't enough to say you were together and at home. I am afraid that you will both have to remain here for the time being. I shall want to talk to you again, before long. It is also my duty to inform you that I am in possession of a search warrant and I am now going to your house. After that, I may have more questions to put to you."

Edward said, "My wife and I have nothing to hide."

But there was a shake in his voice.

"Do you think we shall find it?" asked Barry as they drove out to the house on the cliffs.

"Anne Winter's key? I shall be surprised if we do. They are a prize pair, those two, but I don't think they are murderers. To do Hardwick justice, I think he would have rigged up a better alibi than that. She wouldn't, though. She has a pretty face and nothing much behind it."

"Except a deal of spite against my sister."

Longton nodded.

"Your sister's an unlucky woman."

Here we go, thought Barry. He's still after Geoffrey.

They completed the rest of the way in silence.

There was remarkably little clutter in the Hardwicks' home. It was an architect's dream house—"Nightmare," muttered Longton, who was traditional-minded, not to say hidebound—and the interior had been done by someone who knew his job. But the whole effect was of a stage-set, not a place to live. Barry preferred a house which might not be scrupulously tidy, but which took its character from the happy family within it.

And there was no sign of the key to the flat in Ealing.

"Not a ruddy thing," grunted Longton, seating himself at the desk in Edward's study. "These people don't even keep letters lying about. Oh, yes they do, though. Take a look at that, Sergeant. That looks like the answer to one little problem, though it is hardly one of ours."

Barry read through the proffered letter.

"I wonder how Hardwick got hold of this? Setting up as landed gentry in Ireland, by the looks of it," Longton grinned. "Georgian house, broad acres, salmon fishing, and the Hunt, too, I shouldn't wonder. Question is, where was the money coming from?"

"Ill-gotten gains from selling secrets. Geoffrey would like to see this."

"He's going to be too busy to bother about that. But I expect the other directors would like to know about it. You can pass on the name of that estate agent if you feel like it. They can make their own inquiries."

"You are still going after Geoffrey Lennard, sir?"

"It all points to him. Anne Winter couldn't make up her mind about contacting her family. Not until Glenda Hardwick told her that Lennard was still unmarried. I have no doubt that she piled it on a bit, about keeping her photograph on his desk, and never looking at another woman. She might even have hinted that she knew Geoffrey had been waiting for her to come back all these years. Winter even mentioned it to her daughter."

"It could equally well apply to David Kindersley. In fact, it seems to me that, as far as he was concerned, it was true. From what I know of Geoffrey, my guess is that he didn't bother with women because he was too busy building up his business, and that he kept that photograph of Anne Winter about to remind him of what a fool he had been."

"Agreed, it could have applied to Kindersley," said Longton, "but we happen to know that it didn't. Here we have a witness who spoke to Anne Winter on her first visit to Broadgate, and who admits that she instigated the second one. But is there a mention of Kindersley in it? Not a hint. He himself said Anne Winter hardly knew he existed, much less that he was in love with her, and what was true seventeen years ago was still true this week. No, it was Geoffrey Lennard that she came here to see, and that is what put the cat among the pigeons."

"But surely, sir, it all turns on the paternity of the child. If Geoffrey were the father, I can't see why he shouldn't have married her."

"As I hinted to you once before, perhaps he did, though I admit that so far we have come up with nothing on that. We are no nearer to knowing what happened seventeen years ago than we were the first day we arrived here. And, in my opinion, we're not likely to get much farther on that. No, Sergeant, I think we've been barking up the wrong tree. We have the second murder to account for. If Winter's murder hinges on the paternity of the child, then Seldon's murder doesn't make sense. Suppose Seldon was murdered for profit? Then Lennard is bang in the middle of the picture. There must be some way of interpreting Anne Winter's murder in the light of that."

They were interrupted by the telephone bell. Barry answered it. Then he covered the receiver with his hand.

"Message from Superintendent Marsh, sir. He wants us to meet him out at a place called Saxon Park. He's got another body."

*   *   *

The ringing of the phone roused Rosalind from her doze. She sat up quickly and the Sunday newspapers cascaded to the floor. She had not meant to drop off.

She hated going to sleep during the daytime, but sheer weariness and her lunch had conspired against her.

Geoffrey was already on his feet.

"I'll answer it," he said. "No need for you to get up."

For a moment, she listened alertly, in case he should call her to take the call. Geoffrey spoke briefly, to some unknown, then she heard the tinkle of the receiver as it was replaced.

She glanced out of the window. The sky was heavily overcast now. There was going to be a storm. She hoped Sally would not be caught in it. The child had gone out, straight after lunch, invited unexpectedly by the mother of one of her schoolfriends, to make one of a beach party.

Geoffrey came back. He had slipped on his jacket.

"That was David," he said. "He wants me to go over and have a word with him. I shan't be long."

She wanted to call out to him to stop, to stay at home with her, not to go near David. But she held back. Geoffrey would think she had taken leave of her senses. David was his best friend. She couldn't say to him that she suspected David of being a double murderer, who had killed first Anne, then Richard Seldon, in his determination to keep his position in the factory which was his life's work. And would kill again—anyone who got in his way. Even Geoffrey.

Sheer instinct drove her running out into the drive, to call her husband back. But the Bentley was already turning into the lane. She was too late.

Back inside the house, she tried to settle back to the newspapers, but nothing that she read seemed to register on her mind. She caught herself reading over and over again the same paragraph.

She gave it up and wandered round the house. That did not satisfy her, so she went into the garden. She armed herself with a fork and started to work on the uncleared part of the land. Half an hour's grimly determined digging produced a huge pile of weeds and a satisfying section of roughly cleared ground. But she was very hot. The air was still and oppressive. And the clouds overhead were black.

Rosalind gritted her teeth and attacked the next line of weeds. It was working, this physical exercise. Already she was feeling too hot and tired to worry any more.

Then, suddenly, with a mighty clap of thunder, the storm broke and sent her running for shelter.

The rain battered down ferociously, blotting out the landscape, choking the drains and spilling out into great pools in the roads.

Rosalind began to worry for her husband and child, wishing they were both safely at home. She tried to laugh herself out of her fears. Sally was in the care of a woman who would look after her as well as her own children. And Geoffrey was a fine driver, who would take no risks on roads awash with water.

Sally came home, dry and happy, at half past five.

"Wasn't it rotten, raining like that, Mummy?"

"I hope you didn't get wet?"

"No. We were in a café, having tea. We'd had a lovely bathe, before it started thundering. Where is he?"

Rosalind felt normal enough to experience the usual spasm of irritation at her daughter's method of referring to Geoffrey.

"He's gone to see Uncle David. He'll be back soon."

By six, there was still no sign of him. Rosalind, a prey to all sorts of fears, held out against herself for as long as she could.

At six-thirty, she gave in, and telephoned David.

The phone rang for a long time before it was answered, and then David's voice came over the wire breathless, as though he had been running.

"Sorry I kept you waiting, Roz," he apologised. "I was just coming upstairs when the phone began ringing. I've been out all afternoon."

"But isn't Geoffrey with you?"

"Geoffrey? No, I haven't seen him."

"But you rang him, about four o'clock."

"I'm sorry, Roz. You've got the wires crossed some-where. I haven't seen or heard of Geoffrey all day."

CHAPTER 17

SAXON PARK lay on the other side of the road leading to the hospital. It was a saucer-shaped depression in the flat landscape, carefully laid out in miniature rockeries, waterfalls and winding paths, to disguise and make the most of the small area it covered. It was one of the most *private* places in the town, and, as such, much favoured by local courting couples. Holiday visitors might find it, occasionally, but only those who could drag their atten-tion from the front, the pier and the beach.

The storm had freshened the air, and now that the rain had stopped, and the sun was beginning to break through again, the revived plants gave out fresh scents. The drying rocks steamed in the growing heat, as Long-ton and Barry, following a uniformed constable, picked their way along a narrow path half overgrown with luxurious catmint and grey santolina. Longton swore as the brushing plants soaked his trouser legs.

"Not much farther, sir," the local man encouraged him.

"I hope not," growled Longton.

The path sloped down to a little stream and a rustic bridge, then along the stream for a short distance. A group of men was standing under the spreading branches of a beech tree.

"This is it, sir," remarked the constable.

Barry glanced round. They were in a small artificial glade, so contrived to give an impression of remoteness, almost of secrecy. It was hard to remember that a hun-dred yards away was a busy main road, and that they were within the boundaries of a town full of people. The

silence of the place seemed to impose its own discipline.
Not a sound was to be heard from the group by the tree.
But as they approached, a figure detached itself.

It was Superintendent Marsh.

"Over here," he said briefly.

They followed him to the foot of the tree, the group
of men dividing itself to make way for them. The local
police surgeon was on his knees beside the body, which
lay, face down, on the path where it ran under the great
branches. As they reached him, he rose to his feet, brushing the dirt off his knees with a careless hand.

Longton stepped forward and looked down on the
pitiful remains of Edna Purvis.

"Nasty, this one," remarked the surgeon conversa-
tionally. "He wasn't content with a couple of good blows,
this time. He must have hit her a dozen times. The first
or second killed her, but he went on. Otherwise the
technique is the same. Get behind your unsuspecting
victim and—wham!"

"I called you because she's a resident of Parrington
and works up at Lennard's house," Marsh explained
quietly. "If it is anything to do with the other murders,
I knew you would want to see it at once."

Longton nodded.

"She worked up at Parrington Hall when Anne
Winter lived there."

"Did she now?" Marsh was startled.

"So this must tie in with Winter, somehow," Longton
went on. "How long has she been dead, Doctor?"

The surgeon shrugged.

"Not long. But I think Superintendent Marsh can be
more help than I on that. I'll be getting along. I'll do the
P.M. in the morning."

He trotted off along the path without waiting for a
reply.

Longton squatted down beside the dead woman. He
looked over the body carefully, sighed and shook hi.

head. Then he returned to examine the surrounding ground. The soft earth in between the roots of the tree was undisturbed.

"The murderer was careful to keep to the path, otherwise we would have lovely footprints," remarked Marsh wistfully. "One thing, though. We can pin down the time of the murder. It was done during the storm. The park keeper," he jerked his head in the direction of a short elderly man who was standing a little apart from the waiting policemen, "met her on that little bridge five minutes before it broke. The storm lasted the best part of an hour. He came back this way about ten minutes after it was over. And found her. He had the presence of mind to lock the gates, so, while we aren't likely to have the murderer himself, we might possibly have someone who saw him. There were only a few people in the park, fortunately, and we have them here, but I haven't talked to any of them yet."

"The weapon?" asked Longton.

"Over there."

It lay, half under a protruding root of the tree, where the murderer had flung it. It was a heavy walking stick, the original knarled shape of the branch from which it had been cut deliberately left for effect. The handle was worn and polished to a high gloss from the steady friction of its owner's hand over the years.

"It hasn't been touched," said Marsh.

Longton considered it.

"It wouldn't surprise me if that stick told us a good deal. And I don't mean prints, though, you never know, we might be lucky. I wouldn't know where to go and buy a stick like that. Except possibly in an antique shop. But I would know exactly where I would be likely to *find* one. I guarantee you could put your hand on one of these in any of the country houses round here which haven't been sold up. This is a gentleman's—and I mean that word in its old sense—stick, the sort they favoured seventy or eighty years ago. Now, which of our suspects comes from a 'country house' background?"

"Anne Winter's own family," Barry pointed out, instantly.

"And Geoffrey Lennard," said Longton softly. "He sold up his place when he decided to start the factory, but that doesn't mean he didn't keep things out of it. Especially things like his father's favourite walking stick."

"*If* it's his, anyone could have taken it. I expect they all knew he had it."

Longton wagged his head.

"That cuts both ways, doesn't it? If it belonged to the Colonel, or, say, to Seldon, he could have pinched it, couldn't he, just as if it was his, someone else would have helped themselves. No use our speculating about that. It's a matter for defending counsel, and they might be glad of the tip, if they haven't thought of it first," he added.

Barry clamped his lips together to prevent him making a bad situation positively disastrous. He felt Superintendent Marsh's interested gaze on him.

Longton got to his feet.

"Now we'll have a word with those people you've rounded up," he said, rubbing his hands together.

There was a flustered little group seated on benches near the main entrance to the park, and watched over by a couple of constables. They looked up eagerly when the three detectives approached, impatient at being detained, bursting with curiosity, and, on the whole, anxious not to be "mixed up" with the police.

But they were a disappointment. All except one couple, who had seen Edna Purvis enter the park.

"What time was this?" asked Longton.

"Just about four o'clock," supplied the boy, an alert youth, with a shock of uncontrollable red hair. "She'd been to the hospital, too."

"Too?" echoed Longton sharply.

"Sandra, that is, Miss Parton," the boy replied, blush-

ing at the slip of the tongue and ignoring Sandra's frown
at being dragged into the affair, "she'd been visiting her
auntie at the hospital. I met her out. I was a bit early,
hanging round like, when this woman came out. Since I
was early, I thought I had time to give my mate a ring,
and there's a phone box right by the hospital gates. I
goes over to it, then this old party nips down the steps
and gets in the box in front of me. That's how I noticed
her. I was a bit narked, like. By the time she hung up,
the visitors were all leaving the hospital, and I'd missed
my chance."

"So Mrs Purvis made a phone call. Then what?"

"She crossed the road and went into the park. We
were just behind her."

"Was she alone?"

The boy nodded.

"She went off down one path and we took another.
We didn't see her again."

"So," mused Longton, when the couple had been
despatched in a police car, to make a proper statement,
"Purvis made an appointment and then went into the
park to wait for him to come. And we can guess who it
was, too."

"Are we going straight out there?" asked Barry, trying to keep his voice to an official disinterest.

"No, not for the moment. I tried that before, remember, when Seldon was killed. And it didn't work. No, I
want that stick examined first. And one or two other
things. But I can tell you this," he added, as they reached
their own car, "he's losing his nerve. That rain of blows."
Longton shook his head over it. "And choosing a distinctive weapon like that stick. I don't suppose he stopped
to think that we might be able to trace it. I reckon he's
reached the stage where he can't think at all now. Only
strike blindly where he sees danger threaten him."

They drove down to the police station in the centre of
the town. As they approached it, Longton's exposition of

the case, which was sad hearing to Barry's ears, was interrupted by a horde of flying motor-bikes, which buzzed in and out of the traffic, careless of the havoc their passage caused. As drivers were forced to stamp on brakes, and resorted to angry shouts and blowing of horns, the riders, youths with wild faces, turned and yelled defiance.

"Young idiots," commented Longton. "I hope Marsh rounds them up and sticks them in the cells for the night. The whole lot of them."

As he spoke, Superintendent Marsh's car, which had been following them, pulled out from the main stream of traffic, headlights blazing and siren yowling, and sped after the youths.

"Marsh is going to be busy," said Longton with satisfaction. There was a fair chance that he would be up most of the night himself and it was comforting to think that others would share his fate.

They found the dead woman's husband waiting for them at the police station. In life Tom Purvis had taken his wife for granted. Now that it was too late, he was beginning to appreciate her. The future stretched out before him, very black. Tom felt very sorry for himself. How was he going to manage without Edna? It was her own fault too, not having the sense to keep out of things which did not concern her.

"She was soft about that Anne Winter," he grumbled to the Scotland Yard men, an old jealousy coming to the surface. "Thought the world of her, she did. That's why she wouldn't stay on at the Hall, though the money was good. Edna reckoned Mrs Winter had driven her daughter away. She couldn't abide Mrs Winter ever after that."

"How did she take the news of the murder? Upset her?"

Tom nodded.

"I'll say it did. Moped about all over the place, till I got fed up. Proper week it's been, what with my mother having her stroke and all."

"Did she talk to you about it at all?"

Tom looked at the floor.

"We never had much time for conversation, like, Edna and me. Of an evening, by the time I was home from the pub, she'd be in bed and asleep, as like as not. Except Wednesday night, of course, when Ma was took bad. Up all night then, she was."

"Would you have said she was just grieving for Miss Winter, or was there more to it than that?"

Tom's conscience, so rarely roused to action as to be almost moribund, wrestled with his desire to "keep out of things". The struggle showed on his face. But under Longton's intimidating eye, conscience won.

"She did say summat about you lot being on the wrong track and if no one else would speak out, she would have to," he muttered.

No matter how they pressed him, Tom Purvis would commit himself no further.

"She didn't tell me, and to tell you the truth, I don't suppose I'd have listened to her if she had," he admitted desolately. "She went up to Lennard's place the day the body was found, and she seemed a bit better after that, but it didn't last. Yesterday, you could hardly get a word out of her, and today, she was thinking so hard, I don't think she heard a word any of us said."

They sent him home.

"So," said Longton, "if Edna Purvis was as fond of Anne Winter as all that, the chances are that she knew who was the father of the child, or, at any rate, could make a good guess."

"You think the motive for the murders lies in that, after all, sir?" asked Barry quietly.

"It must do."

"But where does Seldon fit in?"

"At the moment, I don't know," admitted the Superintendent. "But to get back to Mrs Purvis, she went up to see Lennard the day after the murder and he must have convinced her that he was not responsible for it. But between then and yesterday, she must have discovered something which shook her faith in him. She works up there. She must have chanced on something. But she can't have been absolutely sure, so she thinks about it, trying to decide what to do. Then, this afternoon, she made up her mind. She would give him a chance to explain, but obviously she wouldn't want to face him with it in front of his wife. So, when she comes out of the hospital this afternoon, she phones him, and he agrees to meet her in the park."

"It could apply to others as well as Geoffrey Lennard," Barry insisted stubbornly.

"We'll check them all. We can forget the Hardwicks. They were here at the time of the murder. I never fancied them much, anyway. So it boils down to the Winter family, Kindersley, Maynard and Lennard himself. Quite a cosy little party. Not an outsider left. I wonder when we will get a report from the laboratory about that stick."

It was waiting for them when they returned, three-quarters of an hour later, from interviewing David and Peter. Barry's heart was heavy. Longton was building a wall of evidence against Geoffrey. True, it was all circumstantial evidence, but the work was being done by a master hand. Longton never set anything before a judge and jury that wasn't proof against all tests. In fairness, Barry had to admit that the Superintendent was careful. He neglected nothing.

These two interviews had done nothing to knock a brick off Longton's wall, either. David Kindersley said he was out walking, and had taken shelter from the storm in one of the shelters along the cliffs. It was crowded with strangers, who might or might not be traced. You can't lose on that sort of alibi, thought Barry glumly. If no one remembers you, then it was because of the crowd. If someone thinks he does, you are quids in. It might not be conclusive proof that you weren't elsewhere bashing an old woman on the head, but it would be difficult to disprove, under any circumstances.

Peter Maynard and the devoted Mrs Jones both swore that he had not gone out that afternoon, and he certainly could not have gone to Saxon Park, the other end of the town, without some form of transport. And his car was still at the factory. Even if he could have slipped past Mrs Jones's vigilance, from her ground-floor room looking out over the entrance to the flats, he could never have been there and back in the time, on foot or by public transport, or even by taxi. For Mrs Jones would swear that she had spoken with him at a quarter to four, and later he had rung down to ask her to get him some cigarettes. She remembered that it was five o'clock. She'd glanced at the clock as she slipped out to knock at the back door of the local shop.

In face of the report on the stick which had killed Edna Purvis, even Barry's faith in Geoffrey was shaken.

"There can't be any doubt," Longton told him, with a trace of sympathy, "the stick had been carefully wiped, no doubt before he set out, for there are smudges which look like traces of gloves on it. But he overlooked that little brass ferrule at the end. I suppose sometime it came off and he had to stick it on again. However that may be, there is a thumb print on it. It's a clear one, and it belongs to Geoffrey Lennard."

"It could have been taken from his house," suggested Barry.

The drive to Parrington was too short for Barry to put his thoughts in order. The worst was going to happen. Unless Geoffrey could come up with a cast-iron alibi for the time of the murder. Barry found himself praying that he would.

But Geoffrey wasn't even there.

Sally came running out when she heard the car in the drive. Her face dropped when she saw who it was, and she vanished round the side of the house.

Rosalind's face told its own story of worry.

"I'm afraid he is not here, Superintendent. I don't know what time he will be back."

"What time did he go out?"

"Shortly after four."

"In response to a telephone call?"

Rosalind's face went a shade paler.

"How did you know?"

Another car turned in from the lane, and this time it was the Bentley. Sally darted round the side of the house, like an arrow, and flung herself in Geoffrey's arms. He hugged her briefly and put her down. Then he faced the detectives.

"You received a telephone call this afternoon?" asked Longton.

Geoffrey nodded.

"Who was it?"

"David Kindersley. Asking me to go over and see him. He said he had some fresh information over the source of the information leak at the factory."

"And did you see him?"

Geoffrey frowned.

"No. When I reached his place, he wasn't there."

"So, what did you do?"

"I drove around for a bit. You see, Superintendent, I have my own suspicions as to that leak. But so far I haven't been able to bring myself to tackle her."

"Her?"

"I think it is Miss Summers. But I have no direct proof. That is why I haven't said anything. She is an employee of long standing, and I find the thought that she could steal our secrets very hard to grasp."

"Where did you go, on this drive of yours?"

"Oh, around the town. I went to the road where she lives, but even then I couldn't bring myself to knock on her door. Then the storm broke, and I sat it out in the car. After that I went back to David's place, but he still wasn't there. I've been driving round since, trying to decide how to tackle Miss Summers."

"And where does she live?"

"In Broadgate. Near the hospital."

"And near Saxon Park?"

"The road borders one side of the park. The other side from the main gate."

Longton said slowly, "Yes, you would have to admit being there. That car of yours is distinctive. People would notice it parked there, even in a storm."

Rosalind caught her breath.

"What do you mean?" she cried.

Longton ignored her.

"Sergeant, the stick, please."

Barry fetched it from the back seat of the car.

Longton held it out for Geoffrey's inspection.

"Have you ever seen this before?"

"It is very like one which I have. It was my father's."

"And where is yours now?"

"In the cloakroom."

Longton jerked his head at Barry. The sergeant went into the house, to emerge a moment later, empty-handed.

"Nothing there, sir."

"I didn't think there would be," replied Longton. "Well, Mr Lennard, it looks as though this stick is yours."

Geoffrey's eyes narrowed.

"What about it?"

"It is the weapon which was used to batter Mrs Edna Purvis to death in Saxon Park this afternoon. By your own admission it belongs to you, and you also admit being in the vicinity of the park at the time when the crime was committed. In view of those circumstances, I must ask you to accompany me to the police station in Broadgate, and I must warn you that anything you say will be taken down and may be used in evidence."

Rosalind flung herself forward.

"No! Geoffrey, no!"

He released himself gently from her clutching arms.

"Yes, Roz. Better to get it over. You and Sally go to my mother. I'll join you there as soon as I can."

Calmly, he ran the Bentley into the garage, then returned to the little group by the porch.

"I'm ready, Superintendent."

The three men got into the police car.

Sally clutched her mother, her child's instinct telling her that disaster loomed over them.

"Where are they taking him?"

"Only to Broadgate, love. He's going to fetch us from Grandma's, when they've finished their talk."

Please God, she thought, but *when*?

CHAPTER 18

IT WAS Monday morning, and normally Rosalind would have been chatting to Mrs Purvis about the week-end which had passed and whether it would be a good drying day for the washing. But Mrs Purvis was dead, and Rosalind was sitting on the warm sand trying to make her mind a blank.

In some ways, it wasn't difficult. She was stunned. Stunned by the horrors which had come upon them; stunned by the speed with which a murderer had struck down those who stood in his path; stunned, above all, by the thunderbolt which had fallen out of a blue sky on her precious marriage.

She had waited until the small hours of the morning, for news of Geoffrey. Each moment, she had waited for the knock on the door which would herald him, only to be disappointed as the hours dragged past. At last, her mother-in-law had insisted that she went to bed. And then Rosalind had lain in the darkness, longing for Geoffrey and wondering what had happened to him.

Nothing, her common sense told her. We should have

heard if he had been arrested. At the least Barry would have phoned me. At first light, she had gone down through the silent house, only to find Mrs Wareham nodding in an old armchair in the kitchen. She was still wearing the clothes she had on the previous evening. She woke at the sound of the door.

"Haven't you been to bed?"

"No, my dear. I waited in case Geoffrey came."

"You should have let me. You promised me you would go to bed, too."

"You needed the rest, Rosalind. You must look your best for Geoffrey today. He'll come home, you'll see."

Rosalind remembered with shame that she had thought Mrs Wareham did not care much for her son. It is only when trouble comes, she thought, that you see beneath the surface.

Still no word of Geoffrey.

The early news told them that a man was helping the police in their inquiries. Nothing more. Rosalind drove down to the police station. She met her brother on the steps. He was haggard, unshaven and his clothes looked as though he had slept in them.

"Roz." He took her hands. "I couldn't get in touch last night. I'm sorry."

"What is happening? Where is Geoffrey?"

Barry smiled.

"Believe it or not, he's asleep. We had a very late session."

"What will you do with him?"

He looked her straight in the eyes.

"If I had my way, he'd be home now, Roz."

"Can I see him?"

"Later. Please be patient. And try not to worry too much." He ran a hand over his chin. "I'm off to get a shave. Honestly, Roz, we'll be in touch as soon as we can."

And with that she had to be content.

There was no question of Sally going to school. Broadgate, for all its swollen summer population, was still at heart a small town, and gossip would soon have it that Geoffrey was under arrest. So they had come to the beach, banished there by Mrs Wareham, who promised faithfully to send word if there was any news. Rosalind described exactly where on the beach she could be found.

She looked round at the holidaymakers, the old hands with a week's tan already on them, the new arrivals carefully oiling their pallid skins against the treacherous rays of the hot sun. Sally was down at the water's edge, eyeing a group of children of mixed ages splashing happily. But after a moment, the child turned away, and Rosalind's heart broke for her.

A shadow fell across her, and a body blocked out the sun. She looked up quickly. Standing beside her was a tall woman, as tall as herself, with hair which was once black, now grey.

"Mother!" she gasped.

Mrs Thornley, neat in a summer suit, sat down on the sand beside her daughter.

"Barry phoned me last night. He said you might need help. So I came on the early train."

It was all too much for Rosalind. She felt the tears come, first in a trickle, then a torrent. She cried as she had not cried in years.

"Which is Sally?" asked Mrs Thornley.

Rosalind turned her blurred gaze towards the sea.

"In the red bathing suit. On her own. No, she's with someone. They are coming up the beach."

Sally was hand in hand with a fair girl. As they came nearer, it was clear that Sally had been crying. Rosalind stared at her companion. For a moment, there had been something about her. . . .

She tried to pin down the memory, but it had gone.

Mrs Thornley said: "That's the girl I travelled down with this morning."

By now Sally and the newcomer had reached them.

"This is my mummy," said Sally.

The fair girl released her hand.

"She was down by the water, crying to herself. I thought she might be lost or something."

"It was very kind of you," said Rosalind. "Won't you join us? I believe you travelled down with my mother."

The girl looked at them uncertainly. She was unnaturally pale and there were dark circles under her eyes.

"Thank you," she said, and sat down.

"My dear, what is the matter?" asked Rosalind suddenly. She knew, without being told, that this girl was desperately in need of help. Just as she had been. Still was, only now that her mother was here, it was possible to face her own problems and have something to spare for other people's.

"I shouldn't have come," the girl replied. "It was stupid of me. I didn't tell anyone I was coming. I left a note on my bed for the people I'm staying with. I just wanted to see the place where Mother—" She stopped, closed her eyes for a moment, then went on, "I'm Fenella Winter. I expect you're heard—"

"I'm Rosalind Lennard," she couldn't let the child go on with the difficult explanation, "I was there—when they found her."

"I didn't mean to contact anyone," Fenella replied. "I just wanted to have a look at the place, then go back to London."

"You have a family here."

Fenella's hands clenched.

"They didn't want my mother. They won't want me."

"Don't condemn them without a hearing," said Mrs Thornley quietly. "They are probably regretting very much that they ever let her go."

"There are others, too, who will want you," Rosalind added. "We may not be relatives, but we are friends and we should like to have Anne's daughter around."

Every word of it was true. Hope was bubbling through her. The moment that Fenella mentioned her name it had all fallen into place. It wasn't a memory that the girl had called up. It was a likeness.

And not to Anne Winter, either.

Fenella was so like . . . David.

*   *   *

Barry felt refreshed after his shave and leapt up the steps of the police station with something like eagerness. This would be the last day. That much he knew. One way or the other, Geoffrey's fate would be settled.

He had to take his hat off to Geoffrey. Not many men would have stood up to Longton's questioning so well. Geoffrey was still cool and self-possessed at two o'clock in the morning, when he had informed the Superintendent that he would answer no more questions until he had spoken with his solicitor. So Geoffrey had been taken down to the cells where he had slept the sleep of the just, while the two Scotland Yard detectives had argued half the remainder of the night, to the point where it wasn't worth going to bed. Only by that time, all the other cells were occupied by the ton-up boys who had kept the station lively most of the night. Longton and Barry had ended by taking brief naps on hard benches.

The moment he passed through the front door, Barry knew that, in the short time that he had been out, something had happened. There was an air of suppressed excitement about the place. From the cells, the captive motor-cyclists were kicking up a row, but no one was taking much notice.

Superintendent Marsh was with Longton. The latter looked spruce as usual, in spite of the rough night, and his eyes were gleaming.

"Here, look at this." He tossed a card at Barry.

"Anne Winter's fingerprints. Now look at this."

Barry took the second paper.

"The same," he said. "Where did these come from?"

Superintendent Marsh looked smug.

"From the pillion seat of a motor-cycle we picked up last night, in the possession of one of those lads."

"Where did he get it?"

"He pinched it out of an empty house. The one next door to Seldon's place."

Barry snapped his fingers.

"Of course, that's the connection. Between Anne Winter and Richard Seldon and Edna Purvis. The night Winter was killed, both Seldon and Purvis were up most of the night. Mrs Seldon was taken with appendicitis, and old Mrs Purvis had a stroke. They would both be out in the road from time to time, looking for the ambulance or the doctor. Seldon must have seen him with the motor-bike. Mrs Purvis could have seen them going through Parrington, up to Lennard's place."

Longton exchanged glances with Marsh.

"He could be right."

"Which lets Geoffrey Lennard out."

"Not so fast," objected Longton. "Why does it let him out? It could be his bike."

"Then what did he do with the Bentley? At the time of each of the murders, he was driving it. If he exchanged it for a motor-bike, where did he leave it? People notice cars like that. Especially if they are left about in the street."

But Longton was shaking his head.

"He could have run it into the garage of the house where he was keeping the motor-bike, couldn't he?"

"We can soon check that," said Barry confidently.

The empty house bore ample traces of unauthorised occupation by the ton-up boys, and traces of the motor-cycle, too. But no motor-car had passed through the rotting gates for many a year. Longton, Marsh and Barry, assisted by a stalwart constable, could open them only with the greatest difficulty.

"All right, so he didn't put it there," agreed Longton reluctantly, "but that doesn't let him out. Not yet."

Barry had returned to the traces of oil left by the motor-bike.

"I don't think that bike has been kept in here all that long, sir. The oil is comparatively fresh. I wonder where it was before that?"

Longton swore.

"Who does the thing belong to, anyway?" he demanded of Superintendent Marsh.

Marsh shrugged.

"You know County Offices. It's still much too early in the morning for them to have their eyes open. They will let us know in due course."

In this, he was less than just, for the information was at that moment being telephoned to Broadgate.

"Why not ask Geoffrey Lennard?" suggested Barry, mischievously. "He would know if any of them had a motor-bike. Just because we haven't come across one, it doesn't mean to say that the thing was a secret. It would have been so well known that no one thought of mentioning it to us."

Longton glared, and opened his mouth to blast him.

The information was radioed through to Superintendent Marsh's car, in the nick of time.

*　　　*　　　*

Elsie Summers stared in surprise when Rosalind burst into her office, breathless from racing up the stairs. There was no need to run, but her urgent desire to confront David, and know, *immediately,* if he was Anne's seducer and murderer, drove her headlong from her car into the building and up to Elsie's office.

"Where's David?" Rosalind demanded.

Miss Summers nodded towards a closed door, directly across from the door to Geoffrey's office. The door to the board room.

"In there. They've started the meeting."

"But I must see him."

"I'm afraid you will have to wait. They decided to begin the meeting as soon as they all arrived, although it's a bit early. Except for Geoffrey, of course. Oh, Mrs Lennard—" She stopped and her face twisted suddenly. "I must go. They are waiting for me."

She hurried into the board room. The door closed behind her with a sharp snap.

Rosalind sank into a chair. She would have to wait, that was all. She had hoped to catch David, just at the moment when he least expected it, and surprise the truth out of him, or enough of it to persuade the other directors to postpone the meeting until Geoffrey was released. She made it with a quarter of an hour to spare, only to find that the meeting had started early.

She heard steps in the corridor outside. They halted at the door. Whoever it was, they would be unlucky. Like she was, she thought in angry despair.

The door opened, and there, incredibly, was Geoffrey. Behind him came Superintendent Longton and her brother. For a moment Rosalind stared. Then she was in Geoffrey's arms.

He kissed her quickly and let her go.

"It's all right, darling. Where are they all?"

"In the board room. The meeting has started."

He frowned.

"It has, has it?"

He strode to the door and flung it wide. Rosalind heard exclamations of surprise, then silence. No wonder, she thought, as a boundless joy swept over her: the look on Geoffrey's face would be enough to daunt any meeting.

Geoffrey advanced into the room, the Superintendent close behind him. Barry, bringing up the rear, turned at the door, and winked at his sister.

Rosalind collapsed back into her chair. It was all right. She didn't know how or why, and in the first wild happiness of it, she did not care. Later, she would want an explanation. But the important thing was that Geoffrey was free.

They were all there, in the board room, grouped round the polished mahogany table, each in his usual chair. But Seldon's place was empty. And Edward Hardwick occupied the seat of the chairman and managing director. He half-rose as Geoffrey and the detectives walked in, then fell back.

Stanley Threadwell was the first to break the silence. "What's all this?" he grated. "Don't you know you are interrupting an important meeting? What are these men doing here?"

"You've started a bit early," Geoffrey replied in a wintry tone. "I suppose you thought I should not be coming."

He looked round the circle of faces. Threadwell, self-possessed and brutal; Edward, wary; David, still flushed with temper from the words which had passed before Geoffrey appeared so dramatically; Colonel Winter, pale and composed, the soldier facing the enemy, which for him was the whole world, starting with his own conscience; Peter, still groggy, but looking better this morning; and at the bottom of the table, turned now to face the door, Elsie Summers, the secretary, and Giles Winter, Geoffrey's personal assistant.

"Well, we have begun, whether you like it or not," Threadwell said bluntly. "And let me tell you that we have just voted to call an extraordinary general meeting of the shareholders in two weeks' time."

"The whole thing is irregular," snapped David, "you need not think that you will get away with this."

"Oh, shut up," sneered Threadwell, "we are sick of the sound of that. Haven't you anything better to offer?"

David started up from his chair, but a glance from Geoffrey stopped him.

"We'll argue that one out afterwards. First of all,

there are a couple of matters to be settled. That is why Superintendent Longton and Sergeant Thornley are here. Giles, chairs for the gentlemen, please. They have business with all of you, but they have kindly offered me the first say. I am in a position now to clear up the matter which has worried us here for several months. I mean, of course, the copying of the drawings of the food containers."

"I could have told you who it was," scoffed Thread-well. "Your precious Miss Summers."

Elsie shrank back.

"I don't know what you mean."

"Oh, yes, you do," laughed Threadwell, "and it wouldn't be the first time that you had stolen something from your employers. You thought no one knew about the hundred pounds which was missing from the Westerbys' house, but you can't cover things up for ever."

"I didn't take it. I don't know who did; it wasn't me."

"You got the sack for it."

Elsie Summers turned wildly to Geoffrey.

"It's not true. Please don't believe him. I was falsely accused. I admit I deceived you when I came here. I told you my former employer had died and so could not give me a reference. It wasn't true, but I couldn't tell you that Mr Westerby had sacked me because of the theft. But I didn't take that money. Mr Westerby himself admitted that he couldn't prove I had, otherwise he would have taken me to court. And I couldn't prove I hadn't. But I knew I couldn't ask him for a reference. The moment I saw you and Mr Kindersley I knew I would be happy working for you. And I have. All these years. You can't believe that I would do a thing like that to you?"

"I don't," said Geoffrey quietly. "Don't upset yourself, Elsie. As for you, Threadwell, the little bit of dirt which you have dug up about Miss Summers has put you quite off the track. Well, Edward, what about it?"

Edward's face turned a muddy colour.

"I don't understand," he hedged.

"You could have put us all out of our misery. How long had you had that letter? But I suppose you were hanging on to it for your own special little scheme. What I like about you, Edward, is your loyalty."

Edward flinched as if he had been struck.

"I was going to hand it over to you," he mumbled.

"I wonder." Geoffrey's voice was like ice. "I haven't seen the letter myself, but thanks to the gentlemen from Scotland Yard, I do know about it, and I made a telephone call this morning. To an estate agent in Ireland, who is hoping to sell a very choice property to one of us here in this room."

His gaze passed slowly over them, one by one, as the silence became ever more unbearable.

A voice shrill with apprehension cried, "You keep your nose out of that. It's nothing to do with you. I've had enough of this place. Why shouldn't I go and live in Ireland if I want to?"

It was Giles. His face was white and his lips trembled.

"You think you know everything," he raced on, the words tumbling out so fast they were hard to follow, "but let me tell you this. We're all laughing at you for being taken in. Didn't you know your wife was a whore and that kid a bastard? Fine fool they've made of you. You ask Edward. He knows all about them. He'll tell you—"

The words were stopped by a vicious blow on the mouth. Giles, caught off balance, went reeling across the room. The Colonel, his own chair overturned in his haste to reach his son, stood back, breathing heavily.

"I'm sorry, Geoffrey," he apologised. "You have shown him nothing but kindness, and he has repaid you thus. Part of it is his mother's fault. She has stuffed him up with ideas about a way of life which can be no more than a pipedream for most of us, these days. The rest of it is my fault. I should have known what he was. Now,

Giles, you will tell the truth. Where were you getting the money for this place in Ireland?"

Giles, on his feet now, and standing close to the far wall, as though it gave him protection from his father's wrath, said nothing. A trickle of blood ran down from the corner of his mouth.

"Don't try to pretend that your mother was financing you," Colonel Winter went on, "I know that could not be true. So keep her out of this. Now then, sir, where did you get that money?"

Giles looked round for help, and found none.

"From those drawings," he admitted, and the tears began to roll down his cheeks. "I took your key to the safe."

Colonel Winter went back to his chair.

"He's all yours, Geoffrey. I hope you will prosecute him. For that, and for what he said about that fine woman, your wife. If, as it would appear, Edward Hardwick is responsible for the circulation of that rumour, I hope you will deal severely with him too. I shall tender my resignation from this board, in writing, this afternoon. Now, if you will excuse me—"

"No," Geoffrey broke in, "don't. There is no need."

"You can sort that out later," broke in Superintendent Longton. "It's my turn now. And I would rather you stayed for a while, Colonel. I want to talk to you all. About murder."

CHAPTER 19

THE Superintendent glanced round the group, but there was no need. Everyone's attention was riveted to him. The Colonel quietly righted his chair and sat down. Even Edward, eager to leap to his own defence, subsided.

"We begin six months ago," Longton continued, "when a woman learnt that she had an incurable disease. She took a couple of days' holiday and returned to the place where she had spent her childhood. She didn't intend to see any of her family, but by chance she met the half-sister of the man to whom she had been engaged."

There was a movement from somewhere. David Kindersley, thought Barry. That bit was a complete surprise to him.

Longton's quiet, almost bored voice had not hesitated.

"Anne Winter went back to London. Her condition deteriorated and a month ago the doctor told her that she had not much time left. Now, she had a daughter, a girl of sixteen, and she wanted to secure some sort of future for her. Her thoughts turned to her family. Pride had driven her away from them, and kept her away for seventeen years, but Fenella's future was more important than her own pride. However, she could not make up her mind entirely. She discussed it with her daughter, but the girl was against making contact with the family."

A shudder passed through Colonel Winter. His straight-backed frame slumped a little in his chair.

"What decided her finally was another meeting with Mrs Glenda Hardwick, who sought her out when she was on a shopping expedition to Town. That was the Friday before last. Mrs Hardwick was out to make trouble for her brother. She resented his marriage and she imagined that she saw an opportunity to add fuel to the flames of troubles which were already threatening him."

Edward opened his mouth to protest, but the Superintendent swept on.

"Anne Winter had arranged to take a few days' holiday, so, leaving her daughter with friends, she came to Broadgate. On the Tuesday. Encouraged by certain false statements from Mrs Hardwick, she then proceeded to contact Mr Geoffrey Lennard. Only, Mrs Lennard answered the phone. Miss Winter realised that she had been duped, but she still thought it worth while remaining in Broadgate with a view to contacting her family, and she sought to enlist the help of Mr Lennard. He agreed to speak to her father, and, in the hope of finding further support in case the Colonel should prove difficult, he told his colleagues, most of whom had known her. So her presence became common knowledge. And scared to death a certain person with a guilty conscience. I mean, the father of her child, who had abandoned her."

Someone drew in their breath sharply, but Barry, from his position by the door, guarding the only exit, could not see who it was.

"Scared to death," repeated Longton, "literally. Only the death was to be Anne Winter's. This person could not afford to have her reappear. He thought all that was conveniently buried in the past. She received a telephone call at her hotel and then went straight out to the cinema. So it must have been an appointment for late in the evening. She kept it, and so did her murderer. He took her out to Parrington, to the Lennards' house. I imagine that he told her some tale about being delighted she had come back, and now they could get married, and why not go out to Geoffrey's place and let him be the first to know the good news."

It was only a surmise, Barry remembered with a shock, but it rang so true that the group round the table accepted it without question.

"She was killed in the garden, with a spanner which he had taken from the repair shop at the factory that afternoon. He hid the body on a pile of builders' materials, covered by a tarpaulin. There it ought to be safe for a day, until he could bury her quietly. There wasn't time that night. He could not be sure that there was not some evidence of the paternity of the child among Anne's private papers, so he took the key from her handbag, and went to London to search her flat. From it he took a bundle of papers, which he destroyed."

Once more Longton's gaze swept the circle of intent faces.

"Then things started to go wrong. Anne's body was

found the morning after the murder. Then Richard Seldon, who was noted for not being able to keep his mouth shut, let out a damaging fact. Almost certainly, Seldon himself did not appreciate the significance of it, but the murderer could take no chances. So Seldon had to go. I admit that Seldon's murder put us off the track for a while, since one of you stood to gain a lot from his death. But danger threatened the murderer from another angle. There was a woman who had been a servant at Parrington Hall when Anne Winter lived there. She was very fond of Anne, and she had a notion of the identity of her seducer. She was also fond of Rosalind Lennard, for whom she now worked, and village gossip had it that Geoffrey Lennard was both the seducer and the murderer. Mrs Purvis, who had already been assured once by the murderer that he was innocent, decided that the police must be told the truth about Anne Winter's child, to clear one mystery out of the way. And, since it would come better from him than from her, she rang him to tell him so. He made an appointment to meet her. In Saxon Park."

There was a cry from Elsie Summers. She loved the park, but now she felt she could never set foot in it again.

"I don't know," Longton went on, "at what stage the murderer decided to involve Geoffrey Lennard. There was no attempt to implicate him in the first two murders. It was just his bad luck that he could not produce satisfactory accounts of his whereabouts for the vital times. But for the third, he was lured from the house by a false telephone call and the weapon belonged to him. It is almost certain that the murderer took the weapon from his house on the day the body of Anne Winter was discovered. You were all there, at some time during the day," he added in a chill voice.

Longton looked round, inquiringly, but no one offered a comment.

"One of our greatest difficulties," he went on, "was discovering how Anne Winter went to Parrington that

night. The vehicle has now been found. It is a motor-
cycle, and her fingerprints are on the side of the pillion
seat. This motor cycle was usually kept in a shed in Mr
Seldon's garden. It is quite easy to trace the ownership
of a licensed vehicle."

"Here!" It was Peter Maynard. "Do you mean to say
someone pinched my old bike?"

"The murderer used it to carry Anne Winter to
Parrington, Mr Maynard. Unfortunately for him, that
same night, Mrs Seldon was taken ill. At some point, her
husband was out in the street on the look-out for the
ambulance or the doctor, when the murderer returned.
He dared not risk going near the Seldons' house, with
everyone still up, so he hid it in the garden of the house
next door, which happened to be empty. And there it
had to stay. The next morning, before he had a chance
to replace it in the shed, the body had been found, and
it was too dangerous to move it. He could only hope that
Seldon, concerned for his wife, wouldn't realise it was
missing. But he did. Several witnesses have told us that,
on the day he died, he was complaining about irresponsible young people. What he meant was that he had
spoken to the owner of the bike—who was a young person to Seldon—but who didn't seem bothered by the loss
and wouldn't trouble to report it to the police."

Peter Maynard was on his feet.

"Are you accusing me of killing the old fool?"

"Sit down, Mr Maynard."

Peter remained standing.

"I've been half-dead with a cold this past week, let
me tell you," he shouted. "I've been too ill to go around
murdering people."

"Ah, yes, this cold of yours. Only it isn't a cold. It is
an allergy, which you have brought on yourself by keeping a primula in your bedroom. You have a box of tablets
in your bathroom cupboard which could have cured the
thing in a day, but you didn't use them. Why not?"

Peter sat down. He smiled sheepishly.

"You've got hold of the wrong end of the stick, Superintendent. I only wanted to dodge the board meeting. When it was postponed, I had to keep the 'cold' going."

"But you are here this morning."

"I was told I had to be, dead or alive. Look, I agree that it was a daft trick, but it doesn't make me a murderer. I've had to submit to the most awful treatment from Mrs Jones. Ask her."

Longton's face was grim.

"You put it across Mrs Jones very neatly. But let me tell you that as an alibi it won't hold water. She never actually saw you drink the potions she brewed for you. Anyone can feign sleep. And, in case you are thinking of the phone call you made to Miss Lucille Threadwell on the night Seldon was killed, let me point out to you that one phone is the same as another. Add to that the fact that the telephone in Seldon's house had been carefully wiped clean. The wise thing to do after you had used it to call the girl. Your bad luck that the woman who found the body didn't use the phone to call for help, but ran to a neighbour. So we found it as you had left it. No, Mr Maynard, you were very clever, but not clever enough. I agree that your original intention in faking the cold was to dodge the board meeting. You started it well in advance, and before Anne Winter decided to take her trip. But you cashed in on it when you heard she was back in Broadgate. There was your alibi ready made. Easy enough to hoodwink Mrs Jones into supporting it. You made it clear to us that you were without transport for the two murders which required it, which distracted our attention from you as being Seldon's nearest neighbour. Down your fire escape and over the garden fences, and you could be in his place in five minutes. But the moment we knew about the motor bike that was it. And it was you who ran Mrs Purvis home from the Lennards' house, the day after the murder—with that stick, which you had just pinched from the cloakroom there, ready, in case she couldn't be persuaded you were innocent. It must have shaken you when she came to the house, that day, asking questions. But you managed to convince her that you were laid up and couldn't have committed the murder. So the stick didn't have to be used, then, only later, when Edna Purvis had second thoughts."

"You're off your nut!" Peter's voice was shrill and the beads of sweat stood out on his forehead. "Why should I want to kill old Seldon and the Purvis woman?"

"I don't suppose you did," replied Longton, with what might have been a hint of compassion in his voice. "Your original plan, hasty as it was, was daring, and included only one murder. Anne Winter's. You got yourself sent home from work and staged a collapse on the doorstep of your flat so that the caretaker could swear that you hadn't the keys of your car that night, and his wife could swear she was nursing you. In fact, you had hours to yourself. Your alibi was based on two sound assumptions. One, that we should accept that you had no transport handy, and two, that Mrs Jones would exaggerate the seriousness of your 'cold' and the extent of her vigilance over you. You took a deliberate risk over the motor bike. If there was nothing to call attention to it, if it was in the shed where it had lain for months, the chances were that no one would think about it, and we should never hear of it. You might have got away with it, at that, since no one did mention it to us. It was by chance that it came to our attention. So you phoned Anne Winter, made a date with her for later that night, took her out to Parrington and killed her. You hid the body and rode to London and back. So far, so good. Then you ran into trouble. You could not replace the bike. Then the body was discovered. So you decided to leave the bike where it was. Seldon would be too concerned about his wife to bother about it. Let him think it had been stolen, if he should chance to look in the shed."

Longton's eyes slid over Peter.

"A mistake, Maynard. Seldon regarded himself as responsible for the safety of that bike. He found out it was missing. He wanted you to report the loss to the police, or, if you wouldn't, he would. So Seldon had to go. Two murders now instead of one. Then we come to Mrs Purvis. You thought you had reassured her, but she wasn't happy about it. Obviously, she didn't think you were the murderer, or she would never have agreed to meet you in Saxon Park, but she did need to talk to you. About Anne Winter, and what happened seventeen years ago."

Peter attempted a scornful laugh, but it didn't come off.

"What was that to do with me? I was only a school-boy when Anne went away."

"You were seventeen and quite old enough to give her a child," Longton told him sharply. "I imagine you were one for the ladies even then. It has been your reputation ever since. Anne Winter was engaged to be married. What finer prize for a wolf than seducing a bride-to-be? And she, poor thing, already unhappy about the match because she had allowed her mother to push her into it, fell easily. That's what Edna Purvis knew."

Peter flung up his head defiantly.

"All right, so the kid was mine. Anne knew what she was doing. She knew I couldn't marry her."

"You little—" David hurled himself forward across the table, but was hauled back by Geoffrey. "Let me get him."

"Be quiet, Mr Kindersley," barked Longton. "So, Maynard, you admit that the child was yours?"

"It was only a bit of fun. I thought Anne would have done something. Taken precautions, you know. It was her fault she didn't. But it doesn't make me a murderer."

"Doesn't it? Mr Threadwell, would you permit your daughter to marry a man who had got a girl into trouble and then left her to it?"

Threadwell's face was a study.

"By God! I would not," he exploded. "And if she insisted, she'd never see a penny of my money."

Longton turned to Peter.

"You see, Maynard? Let Anne Winter tell her tale in Broadgate and you would lose Lucille Threadwell and her inheritance. Quite a loss, all told. Now I must ask you to come with me. I am taking you into custody for the murders of Anne Winter, Richard Seldon and Edna Purvis, and I warn you—"

Peter's hands were clutching at the edge of the table. The fight had gone out of him. He turned a haggard face to his cousin.

"My God!" he cried, "You don't believe this, do you?"

"Mr Jones, the caretaker at the flats where you live, Maynard," said Longton, "made an interesting discovery in the boiler house this morning. He found a set of motor-cyclist's gear. There were three important points about it. One, he identified it as belonging to you, from the days—the year before last I understand—when you had a craze for motor bikes. Two, there were bloodstains on it. Three, there was a key in one pocket, which looks as though it would fit the front-door lock of Anne's flat."

"Geoffrey!" shouted Peter.

But Geoffrey, who in younger days had rescued his cousin from scrape after scrape, turned away.

"All right, Sergeant," said Longton, "take him away."

Barry moved over to where Peter stood, like a statue, still clutching the table. He touched him on the arm. Dazed but obedient, Peter moved forward.

No one spoke as they left the board room. They passed through Miss Summers' office, where Rosalind stared at them, her hand to her mouth; down the stairs; and out to the waiting police car. Peter climbed into the back, and Superintendent Longton made to follow him.

He paused.

"This has been quite an experience for you, Sergeant. In fact, we could say it was your case."

Barry looked into the expressionless countenance.

"Yes, sir," he replied woodenly.

"Have you enjoyed your spell as a Detective Sergeant at Scotland Yard?"

Cripes! thought Barry, the old devil is going to get back at me for proving him wrong about Geoffrey by sending me back to the Division.

"I don't suppose you will be one much longer," added Longton, "I'm recommending your immediate promotion to the rank of Detective Inspector." He settled himself beside his prisoner and slammed the door.

Rosalind found it all very confusing.

"Peter!" she said blankly.

"I'll tell you about it later," Geoffrey promised her. "Let's go and tell Mother. And Sally. Did she miss me?"

Rosalind smiled.

"She's been like a lost soul without you. And as for you, I sometimes wonder which of us you love best."

"Idiot," replied Geoffrey and kissed her.

Giles Winter seized the opportunity to slink past. He couldn't get out of the place fast enough. His father was bad enough, but he would rather face him ten times than Geoffrey once.

Edward came out of the board room.

"Geoffrey, I would like to explain," he muttered.

Geoffrey turned cold eyes on him.

"Don't bother, Edward. Believe me, I understand."

The whiplash tone made Edward wince. It looked bad for him. From now on Geoffrey's hand would be against him. It might be as well to look round for another position, he thought prudently.

Stanley Threadwell followed Edward out of the board room. The events of the past half-hour had shaken him more than he would admit. When he thought of the narrow escape his precious Lucille had had. . . . Suddenly, he felt very old and tired.

"Let me know when we can have a proper meeting," he said. Then, on an impulse, he held out his hand to Geoffrey. "I think we should forget that extraordinary general meeting," he added.

Geoffrey shook the proffered hand. The leopard was unlikely to change his spots, but maybe they could come to a working arrangement. Over Threadwell's shoulder, he caught sight of David performing a pantomime of triumph. Geoffrey had a job to keep his face straight.

Then came Colonel Winter, walking erect and resolute. He would have left without a word, but Geoffrey stopped him.

"Fenella needs you," he said bluntly.

The brown eyes, so like Anne's, turned to him.

"Would she want me?" he asked.

"I'm sure she will, and you her, once you meet," said Rosalind warmly. "She's with Mrs Wareham. I met her on the beach this morning, and took her there. Come with us."

They found them in the garden.

"Is that my girl?" breathed Colonel Winter.

"Yes," said Rosalind, "that's Fenella."

"She's the model of my mother," he said.

Rosalind wondered how she had ever seen a likeness to David. Of course, the girl took after the Winters.

"She's like you, too," she told him, and was rewarded by an agonised smile.

The little group on the lawn was not aware of the company. Mrs Wareham and Mrs Thornley, in deck-chairs, chatted like old friends. Fenella and Sally, sitting on the grass, were playing Snap.

Then Sally looked up, and sent the cards flying. She raced the length of the lawn and threw herself at Geoffrey.

"Daddy!" she cried. "Daddy! Daddy! Daddy!"

Geoffrey scooped her up and swung her high in the air.